Will Love Ever Know Me

Tamika Newhouse

Delphine Publications, LLC
9439 Everton Ct.
San Antonio, TX 78245

ISBN-13: 978-0-9821455-8-6
Library of Congress Catalog Number: 2008911400

First printing February 2011
Printed in the United States

Edited by: Alanna Boutin
Cover Design: Odd Balls Designs
Layout: Write On Promotions

www.delphinepublications.com
www.tamikanewhouse.com

Dedication

Dedicated to those who have lost and loved a friend or a lover. Know that true love never makes a mistake.

Acknowledgements

It has been three years in this new business and I am so thankful for the blessings I have been given. First off, let me say thanks to my husband. It isn't always peaches and cream in any marriage, but you are truly my best friend. I know that where ever life leads us, you will always be there for me. I also want to thank my children because you keep me on my toes, you work my last nerve, and you are honestly my best creation.

For those who have helped me on my literary journey I appreciate the continued support in my efforts to follow my dream and my passion. Special shout out to Driven Diva's Book Club, Kreative readers, Lutishia Lovely, Selena James of Dafina Books, The Literary Joint, Devine of Books in the Hood, Tasha of Books and Beauty, and even those I have forgotten to name. I am sorry because it's so many folks and I am sitting here trying to remember everyone, but I can't. But you know who you are and I love that you are in my life.

Shout out to those who keep me balanced like Laquita Adams, Ni'cola Mitchell, Donniel Jackson, Aisha Moore, Raheim Brooks, and Keyonda Pyles. When I say you all have allowed me to talk your ears off and vent I am being modest. Because you all are truly a sister's back bone when I need it. To my designers Chanel Smith and Miki Starr you ladies truly help me stay above the rest. Thank you to my editor Alanna who not only took on the role of working with me on my rise to stardom but heads all projects for Delphine Publications. I appreciate you Alanna and all that you do for me.

Now on this go round I am not going to be long winded I'll do that in my next book. But I hope you all enjoy this book because it's the last chapter of these characters from The Ultimate NO NO, a book that has opened up so many doors for me. Remember when you are done go to amazon.com and write your review and tell a friend about The Ultimate Series. I love every single one of my readers and I pray I never disappoint you.

Muah,

Tamika

Will Love Ever Know Me

PROLOGUE

August 2005

I rolled over on my side of the bed and reached for the sudden annoyance that was ruining my sleep. It wasn't normally on anyhow, but for some reason, he turned it on. Probably to annoy the hell out of me. After hitting the alarm clock until it fell silent, I rolled back over to my side of the bed, not missing the fact that his side was cold and obviously hadn't been slept on. I grunted slightly to let the tightness in my throat loosen. A night full of tears could do that to you, I guess. Soon, I rose up and noticed my white pillowcase was now this off-white, and you could see the stains from the tears I cried last night. I moaned and stretched over to his side where the pillow was clean.

I started to rethink all the shit I screamed in the phone to the man I loved, wondering how he could stoop so low and slip up like he did. As if someone were in the room asking me questions, I started to mumble, "no, no, no." Shaking my head, I was hoping that everything that happened was just a bad dream. *Did my best friend really betray me?* I had to get up and get my mind off of the new drama I found myself in. I wasn't new to this type of thing. From a long-term relationship with my high school sweetheart, Denim, to the one I can't get out of my system, Troy. I seemed to have a bad reputation with men, and this repetitive shit I couldn't stand. Break up to make up. Fuck with them to just fuck with another. I was tired of the routine.

Sinking my feet in the deep wool carpet, I rolled my toes in the cushion hoping that it would keep my wobbling balance. My head was ringing, and I stumbled into the bathroom and swung open my medicine cabinet, throwing empty bottles I no longer needed out of the way until I found what I did need. Quickly, I popped it opened and dropped two pills in my mouth. "This will take away the headache," I prayed, then reached over toward my shower and turned the water on till the steam from it was clouding the bathroom. Then I dropped my gown and stepped into the hot water to rinse away the funk and the pain.

"Where did it all go wrong?" I had everything going my way just a year ago. I had opened my own lounge, Troy and I had got back together, and I had finally told him that we had a child together. It started almost three years ago when my best friend Dahlia wanted to get revenge on her ex from college, which was Troy, one of the flyest guys I had ever seen. But the fact that Dahlia wanted me to date him, make him fall in love with me, and then dump him was a far-fetched dream. I actually thought I could handle a task like that. But I guess all dogs have a sweet side, and a girl like me can fall hard for the sweet side, and I did just that. I would have a love affair with

Troy that would go on and stretch out two years and would be one of the hardest rides of my life.

I thought all the secrets were finally out once I told Troy we had a child together. When my daughter, Nina, finally met Troy, she was almost one. We became the instant family. I think she kind of believed Denim was her dad since he was there from the beginning, but she quickly adapted to Troy. I always believed that Troy had forgiven me for keeping him away from his child for a year. I was worried about my image more than anything else.

Slowly I turned the shower off and grabbed a towel out of the linen closet. Hearing the phone ring, I quickly sprang to my bedroom. I wanted to get it before it reached the answering machine. "Hello," I said, out of breath.

"Oh, so you up, Ms. Thang?" Jazzaray's voice came through the receiver. I was hoping it was Troy, but I was glad that it was my best friend who decided to check in on me.

"Oh, hey, Jazz. I just got out of the shower. I'm about to leave early for the Lyrical Lounge today. Are you at the store already?" Jazzaray owned a bookstore adjacent to my lounge called Jazzy Reads.

"No, I have one of my employees there. I needed to check on you. Max is going to be busy all weekend, so why don't you let one of your managers run the place and take a break? I know ever since the altercation went down with Dahlia and Troy you need to get away."

"Just the opposite. I need to work."

"Can you please stop being bigheaded? We all single gals here. We could hit up Florida with your sis, Raven. Even your sisters would be willing to get down right about now."

"Wait a minute, my line is beeping." I clicked over the line, and before I had a chance to say hello, a female voice said, "Nitrah? Is this Nitrah?"

"Yes, this is Nitrah. Who is this?"

"I just thought you should know Troy isn't where he says he is. Get Nina and get out of town for a while. You know your girl Dahlia has it in for you."

"Who the hell is this, and where is Troy?"

"Just remember what I said. Your girl Dahlia has it in for you." The line went dead. I hurried and clicked back over.

"You know I hate when you put me on hold," Jazz complained.

"I'm about to fuck somebody up," I yelled.

"Why? Who was that?"

"Call Tim and ask him where the fuck Troy's at. I'm tired of this shit. I want to confront him once and for all."

"OK, let me go get my bat and let's pay Dahlia a visit while we're at it."

"See you in twenty minutes." I hung up the phone and raced to my closet, pulling my hair into a ponytail and putting on my running shoes. Enough was enough. I was about to confront the one person I wanted to be with.

A Year Prior

CHARMAINE WRIGHT

Fort Worth, November 2004

Bobby's side of the closet was empty. His ties no longer hung outside our closet door, his cologne no longer sat on our dresser, and his boots were no longer thrown in the middle of our hallway. I felt more alone than I had ever felt before. Since the day I saw him fucking my best friend's sister in our guest room, my life has not seemed to be the same. I couldn't shake how I reacted. I hadn't placed my hands on any other person since high school. I leaned back in my bed and wrapped the arms that now replaced Bobby's, around my neck. I enjoyed the smell of his body right after we had sex. It's a smell I hadn't known from him in a while.

"Char," he said, "you want me to order something for us to eat? Shit, I'm hungry."

"Yeah, like what?"

He removed my head from his chest and stood up from the bed, removing the sheets from his naked body. His dark skin always made me moist on the spot, but for years I had to hide that feeling in public. He walked over and searched for his clothes.

"Damn, we must have been at it hard last night. I can't find my shit."

I leaned over and glanced around the bed to see if I could find his clothes from where I was lying.

"I don't know, babe. Maybe you shouldn't have torn my shirt and I wouldn't have returned the favor." I laughed as he bent over and picked up a pillow and threw it my way, dodging the hit before it reached my face.

"Try again, sweetie. You know your aim is a little off," I teased.

"Oh, really? My aim is off?" He jumped on the bed and threw his body on top of mine. I squirmed to get loose under his weight. "How is my aim now?" He pulled the sheet down revealing my areola and started to tease it with the tip of his tongue.

"Ugh, stop, boy. That's not fair." I tried to wiggle my breast out of his mouth, but that seemed to make him more excited. Next, I felt his hand trail down my stomach stopping on the mound of my opening, and he began to rotate his index over my clit.

My body shivered, and I started to go on an ecstasy ride. "Wait. You aren't being fair controlling my body like this," I whispered.

"How's my aim now, Char."

"Good," I whispered.

"I can't hear you." His groan was muffled as his tongue made its warm, moist way down to my navel.

"It's good, boo. Yeah, right there." My legs fell apart as if on cue as he blew softly over my clit. Next, my leg jerked, and I placed it over his shoulders. I prepared myself for when his tongue came in contact with my warm opening.

"Damn, Char, you taste good," I heard him say. At least, that's what I think he said. My mind was focused on the ins and outs of his tongue as it eagerly danced on the inside of my walls. My back arched, pushing my hips further into his mouth. He greedily cupped my ass and spread my cheeks, gliding his tongue from the tip of my clit to the crack of my ass. I moaned out in acceptance as I felt the beginning of an explosion. I tried to squeeze my legs together to maintain the eruption, but he pushed my legs back open, and I had no choice but to let loose and my orgasm reached its peak.

My back finally relaxed as I started to giggle in acceptance. I loved when he did this to me. It was the best sex I ever had. Suddenly, my thoughts were interrupted by the ringing of his cell phone.

"Don't go anywhere," he teased. I saw him strapping on a magnum at the same time searching for his phone. "Yeah? Who this?" he said as soon as he answered it. "Yeah? When you want me to get him? OK, that's fine; I'll go to your mama's around one. All right." He hung up and proceeded to jump back in the bed. "Open them fucking legs up, Char."

I obeyed his command, and my legs fell to the side as he pushed his size ten inside of me. I arched my back to make him fit more perfectly and started to gyrate my hips into his pelvis. *Damn, he feels so good.* He pounded inside of me for the next five minutes. I could tell he just wanted to focus on getting his climax since I already had mine, so I enjoyed the feeling of him inside of me until I felt him quiver and go limp.

"You are too good, boo," I whispered.

"All right, girl, let me hop in the shower. I got to get Junior from his grandmother's house."

I rolled over on my side completely spent and fully satisfied. *I'm going to nap for thirty minutes, then head to the office.* I listened to him hum in the shower, his usual routine. Then my house phone rang.

"Hello."

"Get your ass up. I knows you aren't still in bed. Do I need to tell Bobby to let you up out of there?"

"Jazz, why must you call me every morning with that mess? I'm relaxing and Bobby ain't here. He's at work," I lied.

"Listen, I just spoke to Nitrah, and we want to hit up the town this Sunday. Are you down, or do you got to check with the mister?"

"You know what, heifer? I am down."

"Whatever, Ms. Goody Two-shoes. I been meaning to ask what's gotten into you these past couple of months."

"Nothing; just having a good time being me, that's all. The new me."

"Yeah, Bobby must be tearing that shit up."

"Jazz, I don't have time for your filth," I teased.

"Well, meet me at Roseanne's, that new spa, today. I'm having Tim get Junior from my mother's house, and then I'm going to be free."

"Oh? Where will Maxwell be?"

"Working on a new business project, so he's busy. Anyway, call me about 2 p.m., OK?"

"OK." I hung up the phone and stretched my sleep away.

"Who was that?" He walked in with a towel around his waist brushing his teeth.

"Jazz just confirming what she called you earlier about. I'm going to get in the shower."

"All right."

"Oh, Tim, order some pizza, will ya? I'm starved."

"What kind you want? The pepperoni, right?"

"Yeah, that'll do," I yelled from the bathroom door. Then I turned on the shower and hopped in. *Yeah, what would Jazz think if she knew I was fucking Tim, again?*

"So we'll have VIP tickets?"

"Nitrah, do I have to lie? Who am I?"

"What are you, Mike Jones now? I'm asking 'cause last time you were a no-show," I complained.

"Why must you bring up old shit, Nitrah?"

"Denim, that was last month."

"Was it? Well, I'm going to make up for it this time. I'm going to be spinning at what used to be MP3. Kind of like a coming home."

"That is going to be hot, Mr. I-Am-Denim-O, now. I hate that you all famous now. But the major plugs you put in for the Lyrical Lounge is always wanted."

"Using me again, I see. So, how is my baby doing over there with whatshisname?"

"You know his name." I rolled my eyes at his dislike for Troy. "Nina is fine. Tierra is in town, and they are over at Mama's house right now. You want me to call your mama, and we set up a BBQ?"

"Hell, no. Every time they do that, family is trying to hit up a nigga for money and shit. I'll pass on that. We can just hang out. I never get the chance to hang with my girl any more."

"I'm sure you replace me with many females every damn week. But that's cool. Actually, the girls and I were going to hang out all weekend. Probably rent a suite and all sleep there too. No kids, no home, no men."

"So that means I ain't invited, huh?"

"Yeah, you don't count." I had to hold the phone away from my ear as he laughed off my joke.

"Yo', Dahlia still single, right? I got a dude I can hook her up with. We can all hang out. I know you trying to act all married and shit, but you can get it in too."

"I'll see what Dahlia says, but as for Jazz, Char, and I, we are all taken, boo boo."

"Yeah, we are going to get it in. Let me call you on Thursday when I get into town. Love you, Nitrah."

"Love you too, Denim. Talk to you then." I hung up the phone and hopped off the couch, proceeded to the refrigerator to get some juice, then I heard Troy walk up behind me.

Kissing my neck from behind and placing his hands around my waist, he said, "Why are you always telling Denim you love him? I can't stand when you do that."

"Denim is family, Troy." I turned around and gave him a quick kiss on the lips.

"Yeah, whatever. I'm still watching that nigga. Where is Nina at?"

"My sister, Tierra, came and got her. They're over my mother's. Why?"

"Just wondering. What are you doing today? Going to the lounge?"

"Yes, in a few. I got some early accounting to do, and then I have a meeting with the staff. What about you? There's a game this weekend, right?"

"Yeah. I'm going to meet with the other coaches today. You're coming this weekend, right? It's the playoffs."

"Not this weekend, baby. I made other plans with the girls. It's been months. They just started letting me back into their graces after finding out about Nina." I briefly thought about how I had kept my child, Nina, a secret from everyone, including Troy. I was too embarrassed to admit to my friends and family that I had a baby with a man who had left me. But once my relationship was back in effect with Troy, I told him about our child, and everyone else. For months, my friends didn't talk to me because they didn't understand why I would keep Nina a secret from them. I honestly didn't want them to judge me.

Rolling his eyes, he said, "Fine, go out with your girls."

I playfully hugged him. "Are you mad at me?"

"No, I'll call up Tim and Robert to go shoot some hoops and head to the gym to meet with the coaches. We'll meet up later today at the lounge."

"OK, babe, I love you."

"Love you too." I kissed him again before running upstairs to prepare to leave for work.

The Lyrical Lounge was only a few months old now, and I was happy to not feel the raft of the first-year curse. My place has been doing marvelous in numbers. Every night it was packed with tourists or locals and the money; well, let's just say I have plenty of that. My connection with Denim, who is now a famous producer of rap music, has heightened the popularity. Local celebrities come out this way now just for the food and entertainment. When Jazz opened up Jazzy Reads right next door, things just took off to a whole 'nother level. She plans to start hosting different writers for book signings and all that other literary stuff black folks like. I would be lying if I said my life wasn't on cloud nine. I unlocked the door and proceeded to turn on the lights, then I glanced over the lounge making sure the night staff didn't miss a beat. It wasn't ten minutes when I heard the front door open.

"Hook me up with a meal, Chef."

Laughing at the annoyance Dahlia seemed to always bring, I walked onto the main floor. "Dahlia, why aren't you at work yet? And why are you all the way out here?" Dahlia lived in a suburb area in Irving, which was a city directly between Dallas and Fort Worth.

"I took leave for the rest of this week. I'm tired, and the firm is working me like a modern-day slave. So here I am to bug the hell out of you."

"Looks like you're bored to me," I said, walking around to the bar. "It's early so no alcohol; take a Sprite."

"Heifer, I don't want no damn Sprite."

"I should kick your ass out, always drinking up my inventory," I laughed. My laugh faded when I saw Joyclyn getting Darius out of Dahlia's car. She noticed my change in demeanor.

"I know, Nitrah, but don't trip. I have them with me for the week. Is it cool?" She knew good and well having Joyclyn here wasn't cool. I hated that bitch. She slept with anything that had a penis, not to mention she got pregnant by Dahlia's former boyfriend, Eric. Did I add to the list she slept with Troy and Robert, his brother. Jo the ho is what they call her now.

"I'll act cordial, but she better not ask for nothing to eat or drink."

Dahlia sighed and said, "OK. Is Jazz next door? I wanted to get a new book today."

"It's open, but I don't know if she's in there."

Dahlia turned on her heels and walked back outside directing Joyclyn to follow her next door. I exhaled when I saw she wasn't coming in. My thoughts were derailed when the phone rang.

"Hello, the Lyrical Lounge."

"And how are you today?"

A smile crept upon my face as I remembered his familiar voice. Unfortunately, he still made me moist. "I'm fine, and how are you, Michael?"

Michael was the man I fell in love with. We have a history that spans just as long as my history with Troy. Troy and Michael used to be best friends. That is, until Troy cut him off because Michael had a thing for me. It wasn't until a few months after I broke up with Troy that Michael and I got together. The relationship was short-lived when he had to move to Atlanta, but a year later, he returned, and we started up again. I still love him to this day, but I chose Troy over him because we had a child together. If it wasn't for Michael, the Lyrical Lounge wouldn't be open, and for that reason, I still keep him close to my heart.

"Sitting in the Presidential Suite in Toronto and thought about you."

"Toronto, huh? Are you trying to make me jealous? I've never been there." A man like Michael traveled a lot. Working for several athletic and sports agencies, he not only saw the world, but his bank account held more zeros than I'll ever see.

"No, just needed to hear your voice to get me through the week."

"How are things on your end anyhow?"

"Work and more work, and you?"

"Same here and being a mother." He grew silent at the mention of Nina. He struggled with the fact I had a child for a few months. But he wanted to meet Nina. I met with him one day in Dallas, and the three of us spent the day together. I could tell he admired Nina. But for the wrong reasons. He wanted Nina to be his.

"That's good, and how is my Nina?"

I sighed at the mention of the word *my*. "Getting bigger and talking. She thinks she's grown." He lightly laughed.

"Listen, I'll be back in Dallas next week. I wanted to see you two."

"Oh, that'll be perfect because you know I'm throwing my annual Thanksgiving party. You got to come and bring a friend too."

"Is it going to be at your house?"

"No, at Jazz and Max's house. Why? Don't worry about Troy. There'll be many folks there to keep you two apart. We're friends, right?"

"Yeah, OK. I'll call you for the location next week then. Take care of yourself, Nini."

Laughing, I said, "you still calling me Nini? I'll see you next week." I hung up the phone not noticing my smile. I hate to admit it, but I still had a thing for him. *But I can't go there. It's Troy, Nina, and me now.*

Saturday night rolled around quickly. I took Jazz's advice and had my manager take over the lounge for the weekend. The girls set up a full agenda. Movies, dinner, spa, Club Ice, and then, of course, go see Denim at Club Taste. It seemed like time went back three years when we used to come to Club MP3. I had my hair down in loose curls. It had grown some since I last cut it. I made sure my dark chocolate skin was glistening with that new sparkle lotion I got from Bath and Body Works. I wore a new halter dress, which fit all my curves that had spread more since giving birth to Nina. I also wore four-inch black heels and a silver ankle bracelet just for show.

Jazz took it back with her ole-school braids like the ones Janet had in *Poetic Justice* but with smaller twists. Her skintight jeans were riding her apple bottom that got most of the attention. She wore a low-cut blouse that showed more than enough cleavage.

Dahlia was sporting white shorts with a cherry-red blouse and her cut was freshly done.

Char had a new razor bob cut and wore a one-piece brown dress that barely covered her ass. I hadn't noticed how big her ass was until just now. The more we went out, the more I saw a difference in her behavior. She was rarely uptight anymore. "Char, when did your ass get bigger than mine?"

"Who me?" Char blushed.

"Ain't this about a bitch. Why the hell you looking better than me?" Dahlia yelled.

Laughing, Jazz said, "I don't care what Char got on. I still look the greatest."

"I'm just trying to keep up with my girls," Char said, grabbing Dahlia's and my hand. I grabbed Jazz's and together we walked toward the bouncer of Taste.

"Hey, we should be on the list. We're guests of Denim O," I said.

"Hey, mama, what's your name?" He was one ugly bouncer. I had to keep myself from cringing and gave him a fake smile.

"Nitrah Hill. I'm bringing three guests." His fat index finger scrolled down the page, and I couldn't help but notice his nails were as black as my shoes. I heard Jazz groan in disgust. I glanced toward her and laughed.

"Oh, yeah, mama, here you are. Yo', Roscoe, pass me four VIP passes, will ya?" He handed me the passes as I tried to miss touching his hand. "Y'all ladies have fun now."

"Thanks." I quickly passed him and Roscoe handing the ladies their passes.

"Oh, shit, this place is off the hook," Dahlia screamed over the music. This surely wasn't Club MP3 anymore. Taste was all that and more. The floor was this strawberry Popsicle-type color. It was so bright it looked edible. The colored lights that beamed all over the building gave it a fantasy feeling.

"If you ready for a night of pleasure, let me hear the club say, yeah," I heard the DJ yell. The crowd replied in an uproar. Dahlia got mixed in the blend when a guy walked up to her asking her to dance.

"I'm headed to the bar. Y'all want something?" Char asked. I shook my head no, and Jazz and I proceeded to find a booth.

Next, I heard a familiar voice yell out, "I want Taste to give a special welcome to my lady. My one and only Nitrah. Show your pretty ass, boo." I turned around in shock looking toward the DJ's booth and noticed Denim.

The other DJ yelled, "Hell, yeah. We got a chocolate dime piece in the house tonight. Denim O is in the house tonight. Let me hear y'all say y'all ready for some pleasure tonight." He started to play one of Ludacris's latest joints. Jazz elbowed me and started to laugh. I noticed Denim up top grinning from ear to ear. He held up one finger and said to give him a moment. I nodded OK.

"Damn, Nitrah, you got men that's in line waiting for you."

"The only one who matters is Troy."

She rolled her eyes and said, "If you say so. I got rid of Tim, and you know deep down, Tim and Troy is like a double-sided mirror. You'll see the same shit."

"Jazz, not right now. It ain't like Denim is any different."

"OK, you got a point there." We located a booth near the bar, and I noticed Char heavily flirting with a very fine-looking man. And he was six feet tall.

"Jazz, what has gotten into Char? Have you seen Bobby lately?"

"No, I wondered that same thing. It's been a few months. But things must be good, because she sure is happy."

"And changed. I sometimes miss the person who stomped on all of our fun."

Jazz laughed and said, "I don't."

"Hey, Nitrah, baby."

I turned to greet Denim. "Don't be calling me baby." I noticed the female flock that somehow formed around my table when he appeared and realized they were here for Denim.

"Can you tell your groupies to back the bump up?" I heard Dahlia say, walking toward the table. One of the groupies called her a bitch.

Denim snapped his fingers and two bouncers came over and pushed the crowd of women toward the dance floor.

"Damn, Denim, all that over a snap? Shit, can you make ten thousand appear on this table here?" Dahlia mocked.

"Only ten," Denim teased. I leaned in and kissed him on his cheek. It was always a joy to see him. He was still sexy as hell. But now he had more six-packs than a pack of Budweisers. The brother was finer than Shemar Moore. For a moment there I took myself down memory lane when I first met him in grade school. Friends like him don't come every day. I was just happy that after six years of dating we could still be friends.

"Scoot over and let me sit down for a minute. I'm going to have to make my rounds around the club in a few."

"You're getting paid to appear here, D?" Jazz asked.

"Yeah, a few thousand. Nothing big. But I would come for free. It's home, you know." He glanced at me with that comment.

"Damn, Denim, you want to get it in tonight, don't you? We won't tell if you two want to go down memory lane," Dahlia teased. I threw my napkin at her.

"It's up to Ms. Nitrah here."

"Denim, stop playing." I gently pushed his chest. When I felt how rock-solid it was, I immediately took my hand back. My vagina jerked at his touch. *Oh hell, what is it with this feeling these men are giving me?*

"This club has changed, D. I like it more than MP3 back in the day." Char had finally made her way back toward our table.

Denim leaned up and gave her a hug. "Hey, ma, who was that nigga you were hollering at?"

"None ya."

"What are we drinking?"

"Yo', Sean, tell the bartender to get a bottle of champagne for the ladies here. It's on me," Denim yelled toward his assistant who I later came to know as Sean.

"Ooooh, a girl can get use to this. D, I was telling Nitrah that we needed to get away. You want to volunteer to take us away," Jazz hinted.

"Where do y'all want to go? Pick a spot."

I rolled my eyes at Jazz. "I can't go anywhere. I have a place to run and a child."

"Nina can stay with whatshisname. I'm sure he still needs to work on his fatherly duties."

"Denim, his name is Troy for the last time, and I don't want to leave. I'm busy."

"No, you ain't," Dahlia butted in.

"Junior can stay with Mama or Tim. Shoot, I just want to see something," Jazz added.

"Oh yeah, how is my homie, Tim, these days?"

"More like you, I might add." Jazz rolled her eyes in annoyance.

"Oh, that means he's a good dude then." Denim laughed and proceeded to get up from the booth. "Listen, I got to make my rounds, but I'll be back. Nitrah, don't leave without seeing me." He leaned in and gave me a kiss on the cheek longer than normal and walked away.

"I saw that shit," Dahlia blurted.

Rolling my eyes laughing, I said, "Saw what, Dahlia?" I always hated when she continued to cuss with every other word.

"Denim wants to get it in tonight. Go ahead, we won't tell."

Jazz started to choke on her champagne. "Dahlia, leave this girl alone. She's trying to be faithful for once."

"Whatever. I see some potential over there asking me to dance. I'll holler at y'all squares later." Dahlia hopped up and walked toward a man who was asking her to dance.

"I'm right behind her." I grabbed Char's hand before she could get away.

"Char, are you all right?" I asked.

"Yeah. You seem eager to get in these men's faces. Everything all right with Bobby?" Jazz added.

Char loosened my grip and said, "Everything is fine. Now if you don't mind."

I rolled my eyes at her obvious attitude. "See, Jazz, something is up with her, but whatever ... She's always been secretive."

"She'll tell us when she's ready. Let's go grab a spot on the dance floor."

I took another sip of my champagne and followed Jazz. I grabbed her hand and pretended she was my date and started to dance. Suddenly, I felt a strong grip grab my waist, and I turned around.

"Denim, you scared me."

"Shut up and shake that ass, mama," he teased. I quickly obliged, turning my back toward him and pushing my butt into his groin. He took his hands and wrapped them around my waist. I didn't know what song was playing, but for that moment, I was in heaven. I felt like I was in high school again and Denim was my boyfriend. *I miss this.*

I stayed this way with him for three more songs.

DENIM OVERTON

Nitrah was looking extra fine tonight. It was hard to keep my hands off of her. She had gotten thick too. I didn't care that her hair was shorter, but it fit her. Full, loose, and bouncy with every step. I could sense the women's hatred for her as they watched us. Her round ass was pressed against my dick, and it hardened almost instantly. It had been a very long time since I had physically made love to Nitrah. She was the only woman I loved, and ever since I was 19 and she 17, we used to be always together. I also couldn't keep my dick out of other women. I turned her into the female version of me, and after six years of cheating and breaking up, she finally called it quits. That's until I noticed her taking up with Troy back in 2002. I tried to be with her again, but I lost to him. I haven't liked him since. I knew of him before. The whole city knew him as Troy the dog of Funky town. That's a nickname Fort Worth was given back in the day.

I can only imagine where I would be if I hadn't hooked up with Swisha House records and started producing for them. Maybe still love struck. It was easier to love Nitrah from afar. Many women slept in my bed every day of the week, but none were worth keeping. I only hoped that one day I would find love again, stronger than what I had for Nitrah.

The DJ started to play a slow jam. Nitrah wanted off the dance floor by now. I led her back to the VIP section, where a few of my crew and some groupies were being hosted.

"I don't want to sit with these folks," Nitrah whined.

"Hey, everybody, out real quick. Let me kick it with my girl for a minute." One by one the crew left, and Nitrah and I were alone for the first time since she opened her lounge a few months back.

"That's better." She nodded her head that she was comfortable now. "I miss you, Nitrah." I grabbed her hand and kissed the back of it.

"You keep saying that."

"Well, it's the truth. Don't you miss me? Not the relationship aspect, but just me?"

"Of course, I do. We were like this." She held up her two fingers and crossed them. "You still my number one no matter who I end up with."

I sighed. I wanted to ask her but decided not to go there. But she noticed me thinking hard and wondered what I was thinking about.

"If I gave up the music, would you be with me and it be just Nina, me, and you?"

"Denim, don't do this."

"Never mind." I switched my body weight away from her and proceeded to open a new bottle of Crown Royal.

She took it out of my hand and said, "Denim, do you still think of me that way?"

I gave her an *are you seriously asking me that* look and said, "Every time I think of you. You're the one who got away."

"Why? You know we're no good in a relationship together."

"We aren't because of me. But I know I can do better if you gave me another chance."

"That would be chance number 15, and I don't think you would. You are who you are, Denim. I have accepted that. Maybe you should too."

"And what exactly am I, Nitrah?"

She hesitated before saying, "A cheater. You may not mean to, but it's like breathing for you."

Hurt by her words I said, "Damn, Nitrah, *that's* what you think of me?" *Don't get emotional right now. Man up.*

"OK, I take it back. I'm sorry."

I proceeded to get up from the table, but she grabbed my arm and pulled me back down.

"Don't fight me now. You got way too much muscles for me to overpower you, so sit your butt down."

"Yeah, Nitrah, what?" She leaned over and tried to force me to look at her in the face. She started to make those funny faces that would make it almost impossible for me to keep a straight face. I laughed out and pushed her out of my face. "I can't stand when you make me like you again. This is bull, Nitrah, and you know it."

She placed her elbow on the table and laid her chin in her hand and stared at me. "Am I wrong for what I said, Denim? Tell me."

"No, it's how you feel." I forced myself to look at her. The club was dark where we were, but her chocolate skin seemed to glow. I loved to look at her face. It was smooth, and with no marks or blemishes, she looked like someone painted her perfectly. "Damn, Nitrah, you are beautiful."

She blushed and looked down. I took her chin in my hand and said, "Don't look away. You should be proud of your beauty." Without thought, my dick rose too, and I leaned in. I expected her to push away, and when she didn't, I leaned forward, placing my lips on hers. I moaned in excitement as her soft, plump lips brushed against mine.

I expected at any moment for her to push me away, but she parted her lips, and my tongue entered her mouth. I could taste the sweet flavor of the champagne on her tongue. She took her hand and wrapped it around my head.

"Denim," she whispered.

"Yes," I whispered back in between kisses as my tongue went deeper into her mouth.

"Push away. I can't push away from you."

"Do you want me to stop?"

"Yes but no."

I took my hand and wrapped it around her waist and pulled her closer to me. Then I took my free hand and brushed it across her face, moving her hair behind her ear. "I can't, and I want you so bad."

Suddenly she jerked away. "Back and forth, Denim. I don't want to do this."

"Me either, but I love you, Nitrah. Just enjoy the moment. No one has to know. Let me take you out tonight. Just us, after the girls go to sleep."

"Where?"

"Our old spot. You'll see."

It was well after 3 a.m. when the girls finally hit the sheets and were knocked out. Hell, I was tired too, but I wanted to be alone with Nitrah. That kiss brought back old emotions. The fact she wanted to meet up after three still had me excited. I was glad that our old spot wasn't far from where she was staying.

"Open your eyes now."

"Oh my goodness. You did *not* bring me here." She started to laugh when she noticed the park we first met at. We were kids in grade school when we got into a fight. I had taken a ball and thought since she was a girl I could bully her. Boy, was I wrong, because her fist put me in my place. She was my girl since then. Always will be.

"You didn't think I would bring you here, huh?"

"Not at all. I forgot all about this place. It looks horrible now." The spot where there used to be swings was now just rusty rails. The tires that we use to crawl through were flat. Instead of rocks, barely any gravel covered on the ground. The park was definitely old and in bad shape.

"Here, I got you this." I reached in the backseat of my rented Range Rover and pulled out some candy called Mamba. It used to be her favorite.

Laughing, she said, "What are you up to?"

"Just showing my girl a good time."

"Trying to take me down memory lane, huh?"

"Well, are we gonna talk about it?"

"The kiss?"

"Yeah, Nitrah, the kiss."

"Can you keep a secret?"

"Yeah, I can."

She smiled and said, "Good, because I can too."

MAXWELL WAYNE

A day at work never ended at five o'clock. I always had a new client to please or a new business venue. Not to mention the many meetings that take place almost every day. I was in the process of opening up Maxwell's Too. I had worked hard all my life to get here, and now at the age of 32, I was making a franchise dream come to life. Everything was perfect. I had the best girl in the world. Jazzaray came into my life unexpectedly when I met her on the stoop of my old apartment complex, not realizing that she was the victim of a crime I had witnessed a year before. She was the woman I had saved. I feel that God allowed me to save her so that one day, a year later, she would be my life saver. And she did save my life. She taught me how to love—deep, hard, and not just with my dick but with my heart.

I was successful in life but hadn't had anyone to share it with. When first setting eyes on me, most women took it upon themselves to think that because they propositioned me with ass that I would just take it. Don't get me wrong, though. I slept with a few. Most I couldn't remember, but I got tired of that life. The fact that Jazz was vulnerable, kind, but at the same time, mean and loud, she opened a side of me I had forgotten. She was going to be the one I ended up with.

I took my keys out of my pocket and pressed the unlock button to drop my briefcase in the back of my SUV. Then I brushed the construction gravel off my new shoes and proceeded to open the driver's door when I heard a familiar voice.

"Hey, Maxy, I knew I could catch you here."

I turned to look to make sure I was hearing what I thought I heard, and sure enough, Rayne stood before me. I hadn't seen her since she left for Washington D.C., over four years ago. The last time I laid eyes on her she was in my bed.

"Rayne, what are you doing here?" I tried to hide my confusion, but I was confused. What was she doing here and on the site of where my new restaurant was being built?

"I'm back in town. Been here for a couple weeks, and recently, I saw in the newspaper about a Maxwell Too opening up this spring."

I tugged on my jacket to get away from the winter's frost. "Hop in. We can talk inside." I didn't want to necessarily have her in my car, but I was curious why she was here.

I watched her in my rearview mirrors prance around my passenger side. Her golden skin was tight; hadn't looked like she changed much in four years. As cold as it was, she made sure her perfect round D cups were visible. She opened the door and sat down. Then she turned and faced me. Her smile showed she was genuinely happy to see me. *This is one sexy woman, and she knows it.*

"So what's up, Rayne? I know you didn't just come to say hello."

She licked her plum-colored lipstick and said, "I wanted to see you, of course. How have you been?"

"Busy, working, being a family man. The normal." I downplayed the fact that I was now five times richer than what I was when she left me high and dry.

"Family man, huh? I don't see a ring." She glanced over at my left hand and skimmed it. *Damn, she is still direct.*

"No ring but a family. So how have you been, and why are you back?"

"I got asked to head-up this art division in the Carver Institute. It was a huge opportunity. Plus I missed my family. D.C. was fun, but now it's back to being at home."

"So you move back in the dead of winter?"

"Yeah. I guess that wasn't smart. But it's not exactly tropical paradise in D.C. either. So when can we hook up? You know, like old times?"

Gripping my steering wheel I said, "I'm not sure about that. I'm busy, and as I said, I'm a family man now."

"Yeah, you keep saying that. So here, take my card." She reached into her bra. With a quick peek, I discovered it was purple satin. *Purple must be her color now.*

When I didn't reach for her card she placed it in the cup holder and leaned back in the passenger seat. She licked her lips again and said, "It was good seeing you, Maxy. I'll be in touch."

She leaned over and grabbed her door handle and hopped out. But not before she purposely allowed her shirt to rise above her panties, revealing the top of her ass. I grunted and said, "Take care of yourself, Rayne." Then I started the ignition and placed my SUV in drive, and I didn't bother to look her direction as I drove off. I glanced at the card in my cup holder and said, "She is not going to try to wiggle herself into my life and fuck shit up." Picking the card up, I cracked my window and allowed the card to blow away into the winter breeze.

JAZZARAY MEADOWS

It was Thanksgiving weekend, and my house was packed. It was my newest home since leaving Tim only a few months ago. Maxwell had bought a beautiful half-million dollar home in the area of Fort Worth called Mansfield. Everything that happened since the day I met Maxwell was like out of a dream. Today was no different. It was Nitrah's annual Thanksgiving party. My house became the location of the party due to the fact I had more space. Life right now was at its peak. I was on cloud nine.

"Jazz, can you get your head out of the clouds and find me that *Ideal* CD?" I heard Nitrah yell from downstairs.

I had the kids set up in Junior's room playing and wanted to check in on them. Nina was the youngest, and I didn't want my goddaughter getting run over by the bigger kids. Once I noticed that they were fine watching the latest Disney movie I ran into my bedroom to find the CD Nitrah kept bugging me about. It was a 1999 classic.

"I found it," I yelled, running down the steps holding the CD in my hand up in the air.

"Oh, see now, y'all ain't ready for this." Nitrah ran toward me and grabbed the CD out of my hand and went over to the stereo. "Jazz, how do you and Max run this high-tech gear over here? Us common folks ain't got expensive shit like this."

I walked over to her laughing and grabbed the CD. "No more to drink for you, Miss Lady." The stereo started to blast song number one and the room went into a reminiscing groove.

Then the doorbell rang. "Max, can you get that?"

"Yeah, babe," he called out. I walked into the kitchen to check on the sweet potato pies my mama had placed in the oven before she left. The trash can that was filling up too quickly irritated me. "Y'all grown-ass folks need to learn to take the trash out," I yelled.

"Being the mama now, aren't we?" I heard Char from behind.

I leaned in and grabbed a hug. "Where's Bobby?"

"I'll tell you about him later," she said and walked over to the fridge to grab a drink. I shrugged my shoulders and glanced at the pies. Seeing they were almost done I turned the oven down low.

The guys were all in the entertainment room playing one of the latest games we women could care less about. I noticed Nitrah grab Troy and lead him to the open area in the living room to dance. I giggled at how he tried to act like a mack.

"Get it, Troy." I yelled out. The bell rang again, and this time, I raced to it. Swinging the door open, I blinked twice at his familiar face.

"Hey, Jazz, how you been?" He leaned in and kissed me on the cheek.

"Hey, who is this on my lady?" Maxwell said, walking up behind me with a joking demeanor.

"Hey, man, how you doing? I'm a guest of Nitrah's."

Trying to take away the shock I said, "Oh, yeah, Max, this is Michael, a friend of Nitrah's." I yelled for Nitrah to come to the door, giving her the *are you crazy* look.

"Michael, hey, you made it. Come on in. We got food, drinks, music, and all that and then some."

"Hey, Nini, how you been?" I saw him lean in and kiss her on the cheek. *How long they been still talking?* I thought.

Dahlia walked over toward me. "OK, I was in the dining room eating, but I couldn't miss the fact that Michael is here. Is Nitrah crazy?"

"Let's watch how this goes down because Troy is now approaching the front door."

"Hey, babe, who's the guy Nitrah invited?" Maxwell walked over toward me placing a piece of ham in his mouth.

"Her ex."

He turned his head quickly in surprise. "Who's ex? Nitrah's?"

"You got that right," Dahlia butted in.

"Oh, hell, no. They bringing drama into my house."

"Babe, calm down. Let's see how it plays out." I was curious to see if Troy was going to wild out on Nitrah, Michael, or both.

"Why are you here?" I heard Troy say from behind me.

"Hey, Troy, I was here to see Nini and Nina. I was invited by my friend here. You know her." Michael glanced toward me.

Stuttering, I said, "Yes, Troy, I wanted him to hang with Nina for a while and catch up with his friends. I think it's time we all stop being angry with each other."

"This is some bullshit," Troy yelled.

"Hey, what's up, bro?" I heard Robert say from the top balcony. "Michael, what's up, man? What are you doing here?"

Throwing up my hands, I pulled Michael inside and closed the front door. "He's been family with y'all forever, and enough is enough. We need to all move on. Jazz, can you take Michael to Nina please."

"Fuck no. That's *my* seed. *I'm* her daddy, not his punk ass. Why the fuck are you here?"

"Look, Troy, I ain't having you to call me out of any more of your names. Look, I just wanted to see my girls, and then I'll leave."

Troy raced toward Michael and knocked me down in the process. I fell flat on my ass and yelled for Troy to stop. Next, I saw Maxwell run toward Troy and Michael. Troy stood only inches away from Michael's face.

"Did you just call my woman and my child *your girls?* You got me fucked up, Mike, if you think you're going to continue to come around me and mines." He pushed Michael in the chest.

Now Maxwell hurriedly walked between them. I crawled to my knees to get back on my feet. "I'm sorry. Never mind, Michael. I'll call you later. I thought everyone could get over this."

Dahlia yelled, "Why would you think it was OK for him to come here? You already just told us about Nina. How the hell do you think we feel about *this?*"

My eyes darted toward Dahlia. *Whose side is she on?*

I was surprised to see Michael throw his hands up and place them on the doorknob. "Nini, I don't want to cause problems in your life. I'll be in touch." He walked out and closed the door.

Troy turned and looked at me, obviously out of breath from his rage. "Really, Nitrah, let me talk to you upstairs."

I followed him up the stairs, not giving anyone in the room any eye contact. *Why was what I did by inviting him such a horrible thing? Michael used to be their friend too.*

We walked into one of Jazz and Max's guest rooms, and Troy closed the door behind me. "Are you fucking Michael again?"

Rolling my eyes I said, "No, Troy, we're past all that. At least I thought we were."

"That's hard to believe since he showed up here and disrespected me like that. Nitrah, I'm pissed at how you handled this. I don't want that man around my daughter. How the fuck does he even know my daughter?"

Not realizing that I hadn't told Troy that I allowed Michael to spend time with Nina I had to come clean. "About a month after we brought her home I went to meet him in Dallas."

Troy glared at me fuming, furious that I had met with Michael and had brought Nina.

"Troy, it was just a meet-up. He wanted to end things on a good note, and I owed him that."

"You *owed* him?"

"Yes, I did. For how I treated him. I had to tell him that we were a family now."

"This is some dysfunctional shit. Nitrah, how many times do we have to go backward? Why can't you just leave well enough alone?"

"I have. I mean, I did. I don't know."

"So what you saying? You still want him?"

"No, I don't. I have what I want, what Nina needs, and that's you."

"Get your shit and let's go."

"Go where?"

"Home. I am not having this conversation here." He swung open the door and stormed toward Junior's room to retrieve Nina. I jogged down the stairs, not really wanting to face my girls.

"Everything all right?" Jazz said, walking up behind me as I grabbed Nina's diaper bag.

"It's fine. We're leaving. I'll call you later," then I gave her a brief hug and grabbed my keys off the kitchen counter. I waved at the crowd not missing Dahlia roll her eyes at me. *I'll talk to her later and see what's up.*

I would have rather walked in the 20-degree winter weather than be stuck in this car with Troy right about now. He was clearly upset. I didn't know what to say or how to say it to make this situation better. I honestly wanted him to befriend Michael. Why, I don't know. It was fun only for a brief moment when we all were cool. It would be Troy, Robert, Tim, Michael, Dahlia, Charmaine, Jazzaray, and me. But, it seemed nothing ever stayed the same.

We pulled up into our driveway, and I proceeded to unbuckle Nina out of her car seat. Troy still hadn't said anything. *My Thanksgiving party ruined; just great.* Inside, Nina took off to her room. I ran behind her to cut on her television before she had a chance to whine about it not being on. Then slipping out of my coat, I tiptoed back toward the front closet to hang up our coats. I was waiting for the moment when Troy would start to go off. I imagined he didn't want to argue in front of Nina.

Ten more minutes passed, and I was sitting at the kitchen table afraid to walk into our bedroom. Troy still hadn't come out to see where I was. I sighed at the division I felt in my own house. "This was supposed to be my happily ever after," I whispered to myself. I didn't notice that a small tear crept out of my eye. Quickly, I wiped it away.

Slowly, I got up and climbed the stairs to my office. It was the perfect getaway for any person who needed some *me* time. I had a chaise custom-made of plush red and pastel-colored pillows accompanied it. That's where I plopped down and reached for my CD player. I pressed play and Will Downing came to life. *Perfect; this is what I need.* Then I closed my eyes and lay back on the chaise, placed a pillow in my arms, and squeezed it. Another tear found its way onto my cheek. It had seemed that since bringing Nina back to Fort Worth and moving into this new house with Troy that everything wasn't perfect. Somewhere deep down, Troy stopped looking at me the same and our conversations were forced half the time. Maybe this was why it was easy for me to let Denim kiss me.

"Why are you crying?" I heard Troy's voice say.

"Oh, I didn't know you were in here."

He stood in the doorway and leaned up against the frame.

"Why are you crying, Nitrah?" His voice held little concern. More like he challenged if my tears were sincere.

"I don't know, Troy. I just feel sad."

"Why?"

"Why? I don't feel like talking." I turned on my opposite side making sure my back was to him. *Why aren't we happy?*

"I don't understand why you're crying, that's all. I should be the one hurt. Michael, of all people. Are y'all fucking?"

"No, I hadn't even seen him. He's a friend. I'm tired of the division. You two used to be so close."

"Not any more, Nitrah, and leave it at that. I'm serious. What you pulled was a low blow."

"How? I'm only trying to mend fences. Why must you hate me for that?"

"What the hell is this? It seems like we are never on the same page."

"When did we get this bad, Troy? We used to be happy at some point." I wiped a tear before it reached my pillow.

Troy sighed. I waited for him to reply, but after a whole minute passed, I turned around and noticed the doorway was empty.

"Gone again." Then I heard the front door open and close. I lay there listening to Will Downing, hoping he could sing the pain away.

JAZZARAY MEADOWS

December 2004

I walked in and instantly my eyes tried to adjust to the many colors that hung from the wall. Toddlers just couldn't do anything but glue and stick. I didn't miss teaching at a day care at all. Junior had let loose of my hand and ran over to Tim who stood in the foyer of the day care center. I walked over to him and greeted him with a friendly hug.

"How long have you been here?"

"About ten minutes. What's up, man? You looking fly today, homie," he said to Junior.

"Yes, Mama has good taste," I boasted. "Where do they have us sitting, Tim?"

He pointed to two chairs in the fourth row. "I'm going to go take him to Ms. Chester, so go ahead and grab our seats."

I nodded and smiled toward some of the other mothers who were already seated. We knew the drill. Sit our ass down and smile through the annoying Christmas program. I noticed as Tim made his way back into the room that the single mothers were up for a feast. I couldn't blame them. Tim was looking extra cute today with the new gear he had on. He looked more fit than when we were together, but I tried to overlook his good looks. It wasn't a shocker for him to get mistaken for the singer Tyrese. He stood six feet, was trim, his hair was low cut, and his beard was shaved into a gold tee, with pearly whites to match. I hoped my son would inherit his good looks but not his treatment of women.

"You looking good, Jazz. How you been?" He sat down next to me, our thighs instantly becoming reacquainted.

"I'm good. You looking nice as always, Mr. Meadows," I teased, brushing my hand over his sleeve.

"Thanks. You know I try." He popped his collar and rubbed his chin, boasting his good looks. I rolled my eyes and pushed him away.

"You still taking Junior this weekend? I didn't mention it to him, just in case."

"Yeah, I'm coming to get my little man. I know what you thinking, Jazz. I'm not lying."

"OK, I'm just saying. So what do you think they have our son doing in this play?"

"It better not be anything fruity. My son is a man."

I rolled my eyes. "It's a pre-K program, Tim. He can be a fruit for all I care."

"Yeah, whatever. So have you talked to Nitrah or Troy since the party?"

"I've seen Nitrah at the lounge, but she's been all work and doesn't want to talk about it. What about you? Anything new going on I should know about? Still treating women as your drawers?"

Laughing, he said, "A tad bit jealous, aren't we? I mean, you can still get some love, Jazz, if you beg." He playfully wrapped his arm around my waist and squeezed.

I unwound his arm and said, "No, I think I'll pass. Besides, I'd rather just stick to the sweet memories."

"Yeah, I do that too."

I looked at him to see if he was serious, then he burst into laughter.

"Not funny, Tim. You're embarrassing me."

He placed his arm over my shoulder. "Come on, Jazzy; you know I'm playing with you. I know how you are."

"Why are you in such a good mood? You got a new lady?"

"Nope, just with the one who matters."

"Really? And who is that?"

"Come on, Jazz, you got to ask?"

"Yeah, I guess I don't, huh?" An awkward silence crept over us as the crowd started to applause. I turned my attention toward the stage to focus on Junior and his play. Tim was always playing with my mind and my emotions, and that ship has sailed away. It was Maxwell and I now.

"Get out of my closet, Jazz. Damn, your needy ass is always in my stuff," Dahlia yelled, pulling one of her new shirts from my grip.

"Come on, you ain't even worn this yet. I bet it's been in this closet for three months or something," I begged.

"I don't care what y'all put on, but y'all need to decide. Hell, I'm bored," Charmaine said.

"Can we talk about Bobby now?" Nitrah asked. We were all piled on top of Dahlia's bed waiting for her to get dressed so that we could all go out.

"Why must y'all keep bothering me about him? We're separated. End of discussion." Charmaine clearly was getting an attitude.

"I want to know why. When we have men problems, we all talk about it like this is an Oprah special, but when it comes to you, it's a CIA classified type of shit," Dahlia mocked.

Charmaine rose up from the bed and started to put her shoes on. "Are y'all coming or what? I'll talk about my failed marriage on my own time. Cool?"

"Fine, let's go. Dahlia, throw on a rag and let's go," Nitrah said following Charmaine out of the room.

I shrugged my shoulders and watched Dahlia hop into some skintight jeans. Then I reached over and grabbed her remote to the CD player and pressed power.

"Damn, Jazz, make yourself comfortable, why don't you?"

"I miss this girls'-night-out stuff. Let's make sure we party hard tonight."

"You ain't said anything but a word. Cut that off and come on."

I threw the remote down on the bed and raced behind Dahlia as we made our way to her front door.

We pulled up to the Rhapsody, and sweet memories started to pour out. The only thing is I didn't have any memories of Maxwell and me here, but of Tim and me. I sighed at the annoyance of thinking about Tim. It had only been five months since we last shared a home together.

"Haven't been here in a few months. Is it ole-school night?" Charmaine asked.

"Sure is." Nitrah turned around in the passenger seat and said, "I know we all older now, and we got grown-folk problems, but how about we reminisce like it was us back in college again?"

"Like pull phone numbers and grind my ass into a dude's crotch. Oh, I can do that," Dahlia said.

"Sure you can, Dahlia. You don't have a man at home," I protested.

"Hell, Jazz, you ain't married to Max, and this is just fun and games. I'm down."

We stepped into the Rhapsody after showing our IDs. We had been coming here for years. Nitrah used to do a Spoken Word showcase here every month before she opened the Lyrical Lounge.

"Ms. Nitrah Hill, always a pleasure to see you come back home," the bouncer said after raising the red divider to let us in. "Your money is no good here. You ladies go in and have a great time."

"Thanks, Eddie," Nitrah said, strutting her way by. She was switching extra hard. *OK, I'm going to try and relax and just be carefree tonight.*

We found a table on the top level. It was our favorite spot to have since we were able to see the entire floor down below. Then a familiar tone started to play through the DJ's system.

"*Poison.* Oh hell, yeah, that's my song, ladies. Get up." Dahlia grabbed my hand and led me down the stairway to the main dance floor. I hated to dance in public, but I decided to close my eyes and let BBD sing about a big butt and a smile in my ear. I bent down and placed my hands on my knees and rotated my butt in a circular motion. I figured this was how the real freaks did it.

"Jazz, open your eyes, girl," I heard Dahlia say over the music.

"What? I'm getting into the zone." I leaned up and looked toward Dahlia, who, of course, could dance the best. I tried to mimic her latest move but looked like I was stroking out.

"OK, girl, just do this." Dahlia noticed my sudden stop. "What's wrong, Jazz?" She turned around to see what had made my entire mood change.

"What in the hell?" I said. My eyes were playing tricks on me. I was *not* seeing this, and definitely *not* in Nitrah's favorite spot. I saw Dahlia raise her cell phone and take a picture.

"I'm about to send this shit to Nitrah."

"Are you texting her? Oh hell, Dahlia, I don't know about that." We hurriedly walked off the dance floor and stood along the wall. It wasn't two minutes when I saw Nitrah pouncing down the steps with Charmaine behind her. This is a never-ending door with these two.

TROY WASHINGTON

I screamed out in agony from the strike on my back. I turned around furious and eager to hit whoever just punched my back. "Nitrah!" I yelled out. I knew this was a bad situation before she said anything. Her face said it all. She was hurt.

"You got to be fucking with me, right? You're cheating again, Troy."

Embarrassed, I turned to Kyra, a woman I met at the gym, and excused myself from the dance floor, pulling Nitrah by the arm away from the crowd. I didn't miss the fact that Charmaine, Dahlia, and Jazz were in the back watching the two of us. *Perfect. I don't need more drama from her sidekicks.* We made it to the patio in the back of the club, but not before Nitrah constantly threw cuss words and blows to my right and left arm. Quickly, I opened the sliding door and walked out.

"Is *this* what we have become? You creeping again, and I'm supposed to turn the other cheek?"

"Nitrah, I'm sorry you had to see me here."

"Oh yeah, my favorite place of all clubs, right?"

"You haven't been here in months, and I didn't expect to see you here."

"That's your reason? Damn, Troy, after all this time. After all we have done to get back together, and you pull this shit."

"Exactly, Nitrah. We did all of that to be together, and for what? For you to tell me we had a child who was damn near one." I rubbed my temples, clearly having a headache.

"What? Why are we *still* there? I thought you had forgiven me."

"It's harder than I thought."

"So instead of working it out, you find loving somewhere else. We were supposed to be a family. We moved in together and everything, and now I see you having doubts about me. About us, Troy. Why? We were happy, weren't we?"

I leaned against the wall trying to hide the furious tears that were threatening to make their way to the surface. "Nitrah, I'm moving out. I need time alone."

I had expected her to scream at me. Or to protest. She didn't. She stood there, her face now covered with tears. Her naturally beautiful face now covered in frowning wrinkles and mixed emotions.

"Round and round we go. I'm tired of this shit. Believe it or not, we are stuck together for the rest of our lives. We have Nina."

"I'm going to be in Nina's life regardless."

She looked at me as if the last words I just spoke cut her deep. "Troy, are you saying you're done with us? Tell me straight-up. What are you telling me?"

"Yes, Nitrah, I am done. I can't get over the fact that you kept me from my only child. I need time to think this through. I thought I could forgive you and move on, but I can't. I hate to look at you sometimes. I just need time."

She grabbed the sliding door and walked back into the club, never looking back. I exhaled a breath and dropped my head into my hands. *I love you, Nitrah, but is it worth all this?*

I turned the power off on my car stereo not wanting Charlie Wilson to sing a love song to me or remind me of what had just happened an hour earlier. I didn't expect to tell Nitrah I didn't want to be with her. But our whole relationship was dysfunctional. From us meeting two years ago only to find out she started dating me as a scam because Dahlia wanted to break my heart. Dating Dahlia back in college was a ploy from my frat brothers. Discovering that I taped us having sex and showed it to my frat brothers was a pain that she still held onto for four years. I guess if I would of never broke Dahlia's heart then I would have never met Nitrah, who would, in turn, be the first woman I ever loved and who would have my child.

Trying to not let my thoughts consume me, I pulled up into my mother's driveway to retrieve Nina. I pulled out my spare key. The house was quiet. I crept to the third room and poked my head into the room and saw Nina sleeping in her bed. My mother took on an instant role in being her grandmother when I told her about Nina. But seeing the hurt in my mother's eyes only added to the anger I held for Nitrah. How can I forgive the woman who betrayed me in the most horrible way?

I grabbed a pillow from behind Nina's sleeping body and lay down on the floor beside her bed. Now would have been one of those moments to call up to God, or say a pray, or confess something to the Man upstairs. But all I wanted to do was just lie there. To try to think of how I can get back to loving the woman I used to love so much. I loved her, but I hated her. Was that possible? I thought about the first time I saw her. Slim, dark, and cocky. A good cocky, though. She knew she was fly, and I knew I had to have her. "Maybe I should have just looked away," I said to myself.

"You okay, son?" I heard my mama's voice through the bedroom doorway. I rose up and walked toward her, not trying to wake Nina.

"Mama, what are you doing up? It's after four in the morning."

"I heard you come in. What's wrong, TT?"

I followed my mama into the kitchen as I watched her prepare her morning ritual. Coffee with cream and a slice of toast.

"So, TT, what's wrong?"

"Mama, nothing I can't fix."

"Now, TT, I've watched your spirit dwindle. Not when you look at Nina but in other aspects. I'm asking you to talk to me."

"It's Nitrah. I can't forgive her. Don't know how."

"Can't or won't? I'm sure she had her reasons for keeping Nina away. But she's here now. If God didn't forgive us for our mistakes, where would *we* be? Son, you act like you haven't done wrong. Now what's wrong with you forgiving this girl?"

I sighed, knowing my mother had a point. But I wasn't trying to hear it. "I'm tired, Mama. I'll talk more to you in the morning."

"Are you staying?"

"Yeah, going to go lie back down with Nina. Love you."

"Love you too, TT."

I went back into the room with Nina and lay down again on my pillow reserved for me. I closed my eyes but couldn't fall asleep. So I decided to just lie there; to try not to think about what I told Nitrah tonight. Eventually, I fell asleep.

"All right, bro, it's well after one so get your ass up."

I reluctantly opened my eyes, trying to block the sun that beamed through the opened curtains, screaming at my retinas.

"Yo', Robert, man, close the fucking curtain. I'm trying to sleep." Forgetting to not cuss in front of Nina, I rose up to see if she was still in the bed. "Where's Nina?"

"Her and mama in the backyard working on her garden. Get your ass up. Mama said you were over here not answering your phone and shit." I leaned up against the bed and rubbed my eyes, trying to contain my anger from my brother, Robert, for disturbing my sleep.

"Get up. I'm taking you to go play ball with the boys."

"Robert, I don't feel like it today. Just tell them I'll meet up with them next week."

"Hell, no. You said that since October. You are getting your ass up. Come on. I got some shorts and some old Jordans for you in the truck. Let's go."

Sitting up, clearly upset, I said, "Why the fuck you pressuring me, dude?"

"Stop acting likes a female and go wash that crumb shit out of your mouth. I'll meet you in the truck in five minutes."

Robert was right. A game of basketball was just what I needed. It relieved some tension that had built up. Before leaving the guys, I made plans to meet them next week. They didn't believe me since I had been blowing them off for a while. But I had to get back to being me. I hated doing this family man routine because I was rarely happy. It was time for a change. I pulled up to my house and didn't see Nitrah's car. I only guessed she was at the lounge. I went inside and grabbed some clothes and shoes at lightning speed, dropped them into the back of my truck, pulled out, and didn't look back. I didn't know where I was headed, but I knew my brother would let me stay with him for a while.

DENIM OVERTON

I looked over and saw that Nitrah was still in a deep sleep. She showed up over at the apartment I leased and didn't waste any time getting straight to the point. It was the first time in a long time that I was inside of her.

I opened the door and saw her standing there.

"Are you alone?"

"Hey, Nitrah, what's up?"

"Are you alone?"

"Yeah, come on in." She walked in a few feet, then dropped her purse on the floor near the door. I swung the door closed and helped her take her coat off.

"What's wrong? Are you okay?"

She started to kick off her shoes, took a hold of her shirt, and began to unbutton her top button.

I raised my hand and said, "Nitrah, what's up?" She remained silent, taking her index finger and trailed it down to the opening of her jeans.

Is she about to do what I think she is doing? That's the last thing I remembered thinking before she started to take steps toward me. Why in the hell did I start to get nervous? My hands were shaking from both anxiety and excitement that Nitrah was here coming on to me.

Maybe it was the kiss the other day. Maybe she wanted to get back together. She took her hand and grabbed the back of my head, bringing me down to her level.

"I'm going to sleep with you tonight, Denim. I want you to not hold back. Can you do that for me?" My dick stood at salute when she asked me that. "Hell, yeah, I can do that," I said to myself.

"Baby, I'm going to do more than that." I took her lips in mine, first brushing them slightly, but in seconds, the heat between us became intense and my tongue cracked open her mouth, making its way inside. I sucked her bottom lip, taking my hands down to her round ass, and gave it a hard squeeze.

"Hmmm, baby, you taste so good. Come lie down so I can taste you down there." I took my two fingers and brushed it across her clit so that she would know I wanted to taste her sweet nectar. I hadn't tasted her there in over a year.

To take away the quietness in the room, I picked her up and placed her in the middle of my bed, then walked over to my stereo and turned on one of Nitrah's favorite groups, Silk. Eagerly, I slipped out of my boxers and stood at the end of my bed.

"Are you sure, baby?" She nodded her head. I took my hands and brought them to her thighs, pulling her jeans down and tossing them to the floor. She unbuttoned the remaining buttons on her shirt and threw it on the floor.

"Take this off."

I climbed on top of her and brought my hands to the back of her bra unhooking it with one hand and sliding it down her shoulders. Her full, round D cups fell to the side, and I took my mouth to her left breast and hungrily sucked it. Her nipple hardened in my mouth. Her loud moans could be heard throughout my apartment.

"Hold on, baby, let me taste you. Open them legs." Her legs fell to the side as I took my hand and ripped her panties from her ass.

"Ooooh, Denim." I remembered she liked it when I was rough with her.

"Denim, what?" I yelled, injecting my two fingers inside her wetness. Her juices drizzled down my hand. "Damn, baby, you're wet."

"Taste me, Denim." She widened her legs, and I knelt down and obeyed her command, first kissing her lips and pulling them apart with the tip of my tongue. I blew slightly on her clit before taking my lips and wrapping them around it. I sucked it until it started to get red. Nitrah grabbed the back of my head, directing me to stay down.

I extended my tongue to its full length and raised her ass upward, finding the hole that led to her ecstasy. I inserted my tongue and trailed her walls, sucking all her juices until I was content with what was left behind.

"Turn over, Nitrah. I want to see your ass as I feel you from behind." She obliged and got on all fours, raising her ass in the air. I admired the roundness of her bottom as I inserted my dick inside her wetness. She began to join in on my rhythm, and I exhaled at the warm sensation of her love.

"Damn, Nitrah, you feel good, baby."

"Denim, go harder, baby; go harder," she screamed out. I held onto her waist and watched her ass jiggle at each stroke we created. Our rhythms were so in sync. We gyrated our hips until we both collapsed out of breath and totally satisfied. The she started to giggle.

I was familiar with that laugh. Every time she was satisfied she started to giggle. I turned and watched her in her moment. I still loved her and now wondered why after over a year we were back where we used to be.

I threw water over my face to help me wake up. Looking at the man in the mirror, I asked him if there was another chance with the woman I loved. What did last night really mean? I didn't know what to think. I wasn't sure if I would ever in my life be with Nitrah this way again. Here we were almost a ten-year relationship of going back and forth, and I still didn't know where we stood.

Taking a towel, I dried my face and threw it across the bathroom sink. When I walked back into my bedroom, I noticed Nitrah was wide awake and fully dressed.

"You going somewhere?" I asked.

"Yeah, I got to go get Nina and drop her off at my brother's house. He's taking her to one of his functions with his new girlfriend."

"Well, are we going to talk about last night?"

"What about it? Look, Denim, can we talk about this later? I got to go. I promise later, OK?" She got up, grabbing her shoes in tow. "Thanks for last night though. I really needed it."

Ain't this a bitch? She's dissing me. I know 'cause this is what I do to all the women I sleep with.

"Nitrah, I head to South Beach tomorrow. I want to talk to you before then, OK?"

She grabbed the front doorknob, opened it, and looked back. "Sure, I'll call you, and we will meet up. I love you." Before I could say I love you back, she had walked out and closed the door.

This is NOT how this morning was supposed to end.

CHARMAINE WRIGHT

I looked through my peephole and cringed when I saw who stood on the other side. I didn't want to answer the door, but did I have a choice? If I didn't open the door, would she then, in turn, betray me and tell the whole world my secret? I decided to play it safe.

Swinging the door open I said, "What can I do for you, Joyclyn?"

Joyclyn was Dahlia's sister and the reason why Bobby and I weren't together. I caught them in our bed. But what happened after that is the reason why she is standing at my door now.

Without me offering to let her ass in, she walked by me as if she paid the mortgage to my house.

"Where's Darius?" I said, asking about her son.

"At school. Don't you worry about him. I'm short on my rent this month, and as you know, I need a huge favor."

Rolling my eyes and tired of this routine I said, "Short again? Oh, what a coincidence. What do you need?" I slammed my door harder than I should have. I was angrier than a mother of the church seeing a hooker in the front pew with her legs gapped open.

"Like I said, I'm low on cash. Do you mind loaning me some money?" She smirked at me.

"Bitch, don't come here with that shit. You know I don't like you."

"I'm in need, or do you want everyone to know your little secret?"

I thought about that aspect for a moment. How would my life be if the only ladies I called my family knew about some of the things I've done? How I used to judge them and point my finger at everything they did wrong? Would they forgive me? Would Jazz forgive me?

"I only have fifty. That's all I can give you. Take it or leave it."

"I'll take it, but I'll be back. How's Bobby these days?" She smirked at me again. I couldn't stand her high yellow ass. Always thought she was cute and got every man she wanted because she gave it up too quick. I despised Dahlia's sister. Dahlia had no idea just how evil her baby sister really was. I knew, and pretty soon, I hoped the rest of the world would too.

I went to the kitchen table to retrieve my purse, snatching open my wallet and pulling out my last fifty bucks. I walked over to Joyclyn and threw it in her face like she was a two-dollar ho. And indeed she was.

"Charmaine, why so rude? Throwing money isn't nice." She laughed, picking up the falling bills. "I'll see you soon."

She walked out and closed the door. I plopped down on my sofa, furious. My angry tears started to burn through my eyes as I tried to keep them from falling down.

Calming down, I picked up the phone and dialed Bobby's cell. *Come on and pick up.* I hadn't called him in almost a month, but now I needed him because I was broke and hoped he would offer me some money.

"Yo', Char, what's up?" I heard him say after the fifth ring.

"Bobby, I need a favor."

"That would be the reason why you called anyway. What do you need?" He had a slight attitude in his voice. The nerve of him since I was the one who caught him sexing Joyclyn in our house.

"I need some cash to hold me over till next week. I normally wouldn't have to ask you, but I have nowhere else to turn to." The phone went silent, and I thought he hung up until I heard him sigh.

"How much you need, Char?"

"Just a couple hundred for some food and gas."

"I'll meet you over at the house tonight." He hung up without saying good-bye. I dropped the phone in my lap and sat in silence. The quietness of my house was eerie. I had just gone out with the girls last night, but I was very close to calling one of them over to keep me company. But I couldn't do that.

No one had been over to my house in ages, and no one really knew the extent of my failed marriage. I had no siblings and couldn't stand my mother, so here I sat. In the quietness of my house. Alone. *Maybe I'll call Tim over*, I thought. But I knew he was busy with work, Junior, or one of the many women he was sleeping with. I walked back to my bathroom and reach over my garden tub starting the flow of hot water. Then I grabbed my lighter and lit the candles around the tub and proceeded to put on the latest Najee jazz album. Wearily, I dropped out of my clothes and sank my body into the hot bubbly suds. My head rested on my tub pillow and shortly, I closed my eyes. I needed to block out the stressful situation I was in.

I heard the knock on my door even before he completed the knock. I was anxious to see if he would show up, and I was up waiting. I opened the door making sure I wore my tight booty shorts and a white tank top with no bra. I didn't want to sleep with Bobby. I did it just because.

"Thanks for stopping by, Bobby. Come on in." I moved to the side so he could pass by me. He still looked handsome. He grew his hair out, I noticed, and now had facial hair. But four weeks sure can change somebody.

"Here. I was able to get $250. Hopefully, this will hold you over until payday."

I took the money and placed it in the coffee table drawer near his former favorite chair. "Thank you, Bobby."

"The house looks the same." He glanced my way. "You look the same."

"Yeah, it's same ole same ole over here." I brushed my hand across my hair as I became nervous. I didn't know exactly how to talk to Bobby anymore. I was surprised I was able to look at him without getting angry.

"Bobby, do you mind sitting down and talking to me for a while?" I didn't want to come off as begging, but I was bored. I needed someone to talk to.

"Yeah, I got a few minutes, I guess."

I sat down, curling my feet under my butt to face him. He sat a few inches away.

"So how have you been, Bobby? I haven't talked to you in a while."

"Everything's been fine. I had planned to call you. I needed to give you a heads-up about the divorce papers coming."

"You filed already?"

"Yeah, what did you expect? I needed to get it taken care of because, well, I'm moving."

"Moving where?" This news just caused my heart to drop.

"Back up to Chicago. Going to head up the family business and just start over, you know."

"I see. Like we never existed, huh?"

"I didn't mean it like that, Char. I just said it wrong. Look, I don't want to hurt you or anything."

"Yeah, fucking Joyclyn in our house was not trying to hurt me."

He rubbed his temples. "Char, don't forget your demons and your secrets. We weren't going to make it anyway with the shit you were hiding. I'm surprised you can look your so-called friends in the face."

"I'm trying to right my wrongs, OK?"

"You know you can only do that by being truthful. Look, I got to run. Look for the papers sometime next week. Take care of yourself, Char."

I bit my bottom lip to keep from saying anything and to keep from crying. I stayed planted as he opened the door and turned to look back.

"I think you should tell the girls about what you do and are doing. Promise you'll think about it."

I nodded my head in agreement as he closed the door. How the hell was I going to tell my only friends and family that I am not the person they think I am?

NITRAH HILL

I didn't want to see Denim, but I knew I had to before he left to go to South Beach. I had made plans to go ahead and speak to him yesterday, but when I got home, I notice all of Troy's clothes were gone. Not even a note telling me where he was going. It was either his mama's or his brother's house. But at this point, I didn't care. Maybe he was right. We weren't happy for a reason, and maybe we should be apart. I was glad Nina was with my brother, and even though she wasn't quite two yet, she was very smart and would have asked where her daddy was.

I surprisingly didn't cry as I tried to straighten out the mess he made by doing a rush move job. I felt a slight relief. The little things he left behind I threw in a box and placed it on the back porch for him to pick up. *Now that's out the way.* Then I sat at my kitchen table in my new two-story house that was as quiet as a tomb. *Is this how it's going to be?* I lived alone all my adult life, but this was torture. I had gotten used to Nina's loud talking and Troy blasting a football game or on conference calls with his coaches. I always admired how he loved coaching his own high school football team. But now, all I had was memories that reminded me that I was alone. Again!

My doorbell rang, so I set my glass of wine down and trotted over to the door, anxious to have Denim over. Truth was, I was lonely.

"Hey, Denim, glad you could make it over." I gave him a bear hug, but his embrace was weak. I looked over it and welcomed him inside. He walked past me and went to the living room and plopped down on my couch.

"Nina still gone? I wanted to see her before I left."

"Yeah, she's with Jailen and his new girlfriend, remember?"

"That's cool. It gives us a chance to talk about yesterday."

"OK, so talk. What's up?"

"Nitrah, how can you act so casual about this? We spelt together for the first time in like a year. We said we were going to never take it there again. Although I've always wanted to, you never did. Why now?"

"Why are you so adamant about finding out my motives? Maybe I missed you," I embellished.

"Yeah, because you always have a motive. Where's Troy?"

"Out!"

"Yeah, something must be wrong in paradise. I get the feeling you used me."

"Denim, you are my very best friend. If we ever needed sex, I would like to know I can come to you for it."

"Not when I love you."

"I love you too."

"Are you in love with me, Nitrah, because I'm in love with you?"

"I'm not so sure. Why couldn't last night just be what it was last night?"

"'Cause I know you. Did you use me last night, Nitrah?"

"No, Denim, I needed you. Simple as that. Like I need you now. You sleep with random women all the time. You must understand me in this aspect."

He turned his body and angrily looked at me. "Nitrah, I just fuck those women. They don't mean shit to me. You do. Is that what you are comparing me to—a random fuck?" He had me there. I had to choose my words right. I didn't want to hurt him or mislead him.

"Denim, no. I mean, I wanted to have sex with you. You're my comfort. But you know us in a relationship will never work. We aren't good together that way."

"So that's it. It was just what it was—a fuck?"

"I said it wasn't, Denim."

"Tell Nina I'll be back in a few months to see her. I'll call you later." He began to rise up from the couch when I pulled him back down.

"Don't do that, Denim. Don't make me out to be the bad guy and leave without us in agreement to what went down. I'm sorry if you feel used, but I didn't use you. It's like how we kissed the other night. I wanted you in that way. Nothing more."

"OK, Nitrah, I get you. Next time I want to fuck you, I expect you to bend over and say, 'OK, Denim.'" He snatched his arm from my grip.

"Wow, that was low, Denim."

His stride toward the front door didn't slow down. I expected him to say one more thing before he left but when the sound of my door slamming and then his truck starting hit my ears, I knew he was gone. *Great! Just what I needed. Him to leave upset with me.*

DAHLIA JONES

April 2005

Four months after we spotted Troy at the Rhapsody with his new main squeeze, I saw him in Wing Stop. Now, I didn't want to say anything, but you know me with my big mouth. I was going to say something rude to his ass. It was in my nature. So here I am walking toward him, and his face is deep into his wing basket.

"What are you doing way out here in Arlington?"

"Dahlia, didn't expect to see you here." He grabbed his napkin and wiped his mouth. "I had a couple meetings with some college scouts. I'm thinking about coaching at UTA."

"University of Texas, huh? So you're *that* good." I tried to sound sarcastic, but I was more surprised than anything.

"Since you bugging me and everything and your head is blocking the screen so that I can't see the game, do you mind moving that thing?" he joked.

I dropped my purse on the table and pulled out a chair. "Got jokes now, don't we?"

"Just trying to enjoy my time alone. Hint: alone. You sure are making yourself comfortable." That was true. Since over a year and a half ago when Troy and I had a heart-to-heart about my hate for him, it has become easier to tolerate him.

And even now it was easier to talk to him. *Wait, I forgot about my insult.*

"Really? Because you sure didn't seem alone at the Rhapsody last year before Christmas." I could see him choosing his words wisely.

"And the Dahlia I know and love comes out to play. OK, so you've said what you had to say. Thanks and good-bye." He proceeded to bite into a new wing.

"So Nitrah and you, what's up with that?"

"Nothing. We're parents to a beautiful girl. That's it."

"That's it?"

"Yeah. Why? Did she mention something?"

"No, not really. She hasn't said anything about you, to be honest. You would think she would have been depressed, talked our ear off or something."

"Yeah, I guess it wasn't that big of a thing, you know."

"Well, I won't hold you too long. It was actually interesting to see you again."

"Is that a good thing?"

"Don't know yet," I laughed.

"You know, Dahlia, don't take this the wrong way, but you look a lot better when you smile like that. You seem to always frown a lot." That caught me off guard. A nice comment from an evil being.

"I'll keep that in mind. I mean, I did pull you and your brother at one point, you know. I got skills." Troy started to laugh so hard I began to feel he was laughing at me and not with me. "It wasn't that funny, Troy." Taking a sip of his soda he tried to regain his composure. He was laughing too hard at the comment for my liking.

I rolled my eyes and rose up from my seat.

He grabbed my hand. "I'm sorry. Don't be catching another one of your attitudes. That was a funny joke."

"It wasn't a joke, asshole." I snatched my hand from his with all the sassiness I had. "I've got to get back to the firm and get these papers over to Steven Francis, you know." I knew he knew who Steve Francis was. He was an influential being in the NCAA. He coached back in the '70s at Duke University and now held an important role with the board of directors at my firm for some leading athletes in the NBA. "He wants these papers before that important mixer with some of the leading people in the NBA.

"Oh wait, you *do* know who Steven Francis is, don't you?" Troy's eyes didn't go back into his head for a good 30 seconds.

"Dahlia, hook me up. Come on. Let me into that mixer. Let me work the room. You said that to get under my skin, didn't you?" *Asking the million-dollar question, aren't we.*

"Hook you up? The man who broke my heart in college, broke my best friend's heart, knocked her up, and still left her? Ha!"

"Come on, you know it ain't all like that. Please, Dahlia, I'll owe you. Do it for Nina." I rolled my eyes at the mention of him trying to bring his child against me.

"Yeah, you *will* owe me. Here, this is my number at my office. The mixer is tomorrow night. Dress in a suit. I'll gives you the address to the place and you can escort me there. But do not tell Nitrah. I do not want to hear her mouth."

He took the card in placed it in his pocket. "You got it. Tomorrow night it's a date." He dropped his head back into his wings, and I cringed at the sound of *date*. That's exactly what this is not.

Last year I had an assistant named Monica who turned out to be Tim's mistress, and at that time, Jazzaray and Tim were still married, so the first thing I did was transfer her ass to North Carolina. Now I had one of the best new assistants a girl could ask for. She brought in my plum evening gown I planned to wear to the mixer tonight and hung it on the back of my door.

"Thanks, Leah. You can go when my escort Troy Washington calls up."

"Yes ma'am. You are going to look fierce today."

"Thanks, lady." I walked over and closed my office door and grabbed my dress off the hook. Tonight was an important night, and I was going to be rubbing shoulders with some of the country's richest men, and I didn't understand why I invited Troy. I mentioned it just to brag and get under his skin, but hell, maybe showing up with him will make me not look like a desperate woman. Once in my dress, I walked over to my full-length mirror and started to brush my hair. My stylist had given me a fresh look, and I was really enjoying my new haircut. My neck line never looked so good. I glanced at the clock on my desk and noticed it was a quarter after seven and the party starts at eight. I didn't want to be on CP time.

I walked over and pulled open my door to ask Leah if Troy had arrived when there he sat in the lobby. Leah's desk was unoccupied.

"Oh, she said you said she could leave when I got here."

"Why didn't you tell me you were out here? I'm ready." I tapped the switch and cut off my office lights and walked toward the elevator.

"Damn, Dahlia, you clean up well."

"Don't flatter yourself. I look this good for the men at the party."

"Cool. I'll just look in the meantime," he laughed.

"Ugh, don't even do that." I stepped onto the elevator and pressed the button for the parking garage.

We hopped in his car and got on Highway 30, headed for downtown Dallas.

"Hey, don't put down the window, man. You're going to mess up my hair. That's what artificial air-conditioning is for," I said, turning on the cool air.

"Black women is all the same, huh?" he laughed again.

"You sure have to laugh at everything," I said a little annoyed. But I would be lying if I said he didn't look extra sexy in his two-piece black suit with the brown vest. I could tell he went to the barber and was freshly cut. His plump pinkish lips were suddenly moist looking. His yellow skin was also blemish free. *It has to be a crime to look that damn good.*

We arrived at the Crown Plaza Club, and Troy gave the valet his keys. Then he reached out his arm to me, and I raised an eyebrow as in saying, *Negro, please!*

"Dahlia, I *am* escorting you, *right?*"

"Yeah, but ugh, do we have to touch?" I teased.

"Come on, I know I'm a little too fly for your taste tonight, but I think you can handle it." He laughed again.

Rolling my eyes, I yanked his arm and cupped it under mine. "Come on, Negro."

"Ouch, be gentle," he teased. I breathed out a sigh of annoyance and proceeded to walk through the motion doors.

The main lobby was gigantic with marble floors, gold interior, and the ceiling went twenty floors up.

"Oh, I see the elevator over here. We're heading to the top floor. The Country Club."

"Oh, cool. Never been to this spot. You?"

"Can't say that I have. My boss will be here, so, Troy, act civilized."

"Dahlia, one thing I know how to do is network. Watch and learn." The elevator doors swung open, and we were instantly thrown into the mayhem of the 20-plus people walking around with glasses of expensive wine and snacks in tow from the servers carrying trays. I noticed a waterfall bigger than my own bed flowing through parts of the walkway.

"Damn, this is nice. All right, Dahlia, hit me on my cell if you need me." And suddenly, Troy took off like a bat out of hell. I temporarily got jealous but brushed that off. *Use me, why don't you?*

I found some of my associates and joined in the crowd. My business cards were in easy reach, just in case. By ten o'clock, I had given out three cards to bachelors who were pretty tasty to look at. By this time, I noticed that I had not seen Troy yet, so I pulled out my cell phone and sent him a text message.

Dahlia: where are you?

Troy: Over by the bar

Dahlia: Did you network good?

Troy: Sure did. Met Mr. Francis himself and guess what?

Dahlia: What?

Troy: He knows the head of the sports dept at UTA and will look at my app

Dahlia: Your application?

Troy: Yes

Dahlia: I'm coming over to find you

Troy: OK

I found Troy standing at the bar with his suit button undone and a beer in his hand. "Drinking on the job isn't a good thing."

"I'm off duty now. Networking ain't easy."

"Yeah, I know. I do this for a living."

"So what did you do?"

I giggled. "I got three numbers, that's what I did, and, of course, talked my boss up to some of the big heads in here."

"Three numbers, huh?"

"Yeah. What's that, low for you?" I said, rolling my eyes.

"Well, compared to my seven, and let's not mention the proposition to meet in one of the private bathrooms, I'll say I got you beat."

"The dog of Funky town is back, I see."

He laughed and said, "I never understood why you ladies called me that. I ain't a bad guy. Just ain't met the right one."

"Still …" He knew I was talking about Nitrah.

"Yes, Dahlia, *still.*"

I felt kind of sad at his response, and I didn't know why. From the jump when I found out Troy, who was my ex, was dating Nitrah seriously, I was against it. The plan was for Nitrah to break Troy's heart and not to fall in love with him. So why, now that when they've broken up and it seemed to be permanent, did I feel bad?

Changing the subject I said, "So you impressed Mr. Francis, huh?"

"Look at me; I can talk a good game."

"Yeah, but can you play it?"

He laughed and said, "Good one. You always had a smart mouth." He took another sip of his beer.

"Yeah, I am pretty smart." I turned to the bartender and ordered a mango martini.

"That's a weak drink for such a fun night," he teased.

"Troy, you drink your nasty beer, and I'll drink my weak drink, deal?"

"Deal." We sat and drank for another hour before I saw midnight was creeping on us and the crowd of old heads with their groupies or mistresses was starting to thin out.

"Let's head out, Troy. We've done what we've came to do."

"All right, you've had four too many drinks anyhow."

I hopped off my barstool nearly tumbling over when I felt Troy grab me by my waist. "I can walk myself," I slurred.

"Oh, hell, Dahlia, you're drunk. Let me get you out of here before your boss or someone sees you." I leaned my head lazily on his shoulder, trusting him to guide my feet to the exit.

TROY WASHINGTON

I did not feel like dragging Dahlia's drunken ass out of the Country Club, but I didn't want anyone at her job to see her. *How the hell she let herself get this wasted?* Making it to the elevator, I pressed parking garage and made it down to the valet just in time to feel Dahlia go limp. *Oh, hell, no, is she asleep?* I handed the valet my ticket after he eyed Dahlia and shook his head. I was feeling like him. A woman this grown should be able to handle her liquor.

Once the valet pulled up my truck, I opened the passenger door and struggled to get Dahlia in the car. I was amazed because she didn't look as heavy as she felt. "Dahlia, wake your ass up and get in the truck." I tried to whisper just loud enough for her to hear. She didn't budge. I rolled her in and made sure to slip the ends of her gown in as well. When I closed the door, I noticed sweat drizzling from my forehead. I wiped it with my handkerchief and walked over to my side, hopping inside the truck.

I headed down Highway 30 Westbound toward Irving to drop her ass off. Then it hit me I couldn't remember where she lived. I reached over and shook her shoulder. "Dahlia, wake up and tell me how to get to your house." I shook her for about ten minutes and in the midst of that time, she told me to turn left when I was in the middle of the freeway and to cross the bridge which was an 18-wheeler's shadow.

Shit, I ain't gonna be able to take her ass home. Names and faces started to run through my mind, trying to figure out where to take her. I could not call the girls because they would wonder why we were together at one in the morning. I couldn't call Robert because he would wonder why I was with his ex. I was out of options. My last choice was to take her to my apartment and drop her ass in my bed, and I would have to sleep on the couch. That's exactly what I did.

Shaking my head in the process, I pulled her legs out first, and then dropped her over my shoulder, carrying her to the front stoop of my apartment complex. I moved here last month after staying with my mother and Robert for the past three months. I decided to get my own little spot because I could see that Nitrah and I weren't reconciling.

Once inside, I kicked spare clothes and sneakers out of the way to make a path back to my room. The bed wasn't even made, but I knew her drunken ass wouldn't complain. She still hadn't woken up. I tossed her on my bed, and I do mean *tossed*. She rolled over to the other side and moaned, "thanks." At least that's what I think she said.

I walked back to the living room, kicking off my dress shoes and throwing them across the room where they landed on the floor near my trash can. Exhausted, I dropped down on the couch, rubbing my eyes to see the time. It was 1:37 a.m. In no time, I closed my eyes and fell into a deep sleep.

Waking up in agony from sleeping on a small couch, I twisted my neck in hopes of knocking out the cramps it was so eager to hold on to. I looked over and saw it was well after ten in the morning, and my stomach reminded me that I hadn't eaten anything since seven last night. Lazily, I slowly pulled myself up and walked down the hallway. That's when I noticed a woman in my bed. *Who the hell did I fuck last night?* I walked closer, trying to remember what female I was with last night. I neared and saw the woman was in her panties and bra. *At least she is fine as hell.*

I walked into my bathroom and proceeded to brush my teeth, trying to recollect who I was with last night. "Dahlia!"

I almost choked on my own mucus and proceeded to spit out the paste in my mouth. Cupping my hands, I took some water and threw it on my face. *Did I fuck her last night? Damn, I hope I didn't.* I could not believe my eyes. I cracked open my bedroom door, trying to see if I had woken Dahlia up. She was still knocked out. My eyes started to trail her body. She lay across my bed almost nude. If it weren't for the half-cut black panties and the matching bra I would be seeing her naked for the first time since college. *Dude, stop looking. What are you doing?*

I shut the door and leaned back against it and looked down and noticed my dick had an erection. *Ain't this some shit? This woman used to make me cringe? Now I'm trippin' 'cause she lying practically naked in my bed.* I had to wake her up and get her out before these thoughts continued. I shook my head as if the thoughts would somehow just pop out and opened the door again. Then I noticed she was lying on her back and her eyes were wide open.

"Dahlia, are you up?"

I must have scared her because she reached for my sheets and pulled them over her body. "Troy, why am I at your place, and did you undress me?"

Walking into my room I started to look for a shirt to put on. I didn't want both of us to be half-naked. "I tried to take you home last night, but you were too drunk, and no, I think you somehow undressed in the middle of the night."

"Did you sleep in here?"

"No, I slept on the couch," I said, pointing toward the living room. I noticed her dress on the floor next to the bed and tossed it to her. "I think you must have thought you were home and got comfortable."

She leaned up and said, "Do you mind?" Motioning for me to turn around, I did and saw a white T-shirt on my clothes basket, so I picked it up and slipped it on.

"Damn, Troy, your place is disgusting."

I turned around and noticed she had on her dress. I was relieved because what I saw turned me on. "Yeah, I don't have much time to clean."

"Well, let me wash up and then we can go." I could tell she was nervous to walk past me as I stood planted in my spot. *I wonder if she is turned on as much as I am.* I tempted her and stood my ground without moving an inch. She slipped past me, rushing into the bathroom and closing the door.

"I'll go pour us some juice and then we can head out," I said at the door.

"Yeah, OK."

After pouring two cups of orange juice I sat down on the couch and waited for Dahlia to walk out. Five minutes later, I noticed her coming down the hallway. *Get these thoughts out of your head.*

"OK, I'm ready. Is this one for me?" She pointed toward one of the cups of juices.

I handed it to her and stood up. "Ready?"

We hopped in the car and headed back on Highway 30 for Irving. "See, we wouldn't be backtracking if you weren't so drunk last night," I laughed.

"Not so loud, Troy, I have a headache."

"Sure you do!"

"So I must have had a ball last night to get that drunk."

"Yeah, and you owe me gas money too."

"What?"

I laughed and waved her off.

"You mind stopping by Whataburger? I'm so hungry."

"Yeah, I can do that because I'm hungry too." After ordering a couple burgers, I drove five more miles to her house and parked in the driveway, where I greedily pulled out my food and started to munch on it.

"You can eat inside; it's pretty hot out here."

I turned off the engine, dropping my food back into the bag. Inside her house I saw how tidy and clean she was.

"This is nice, Dahlia."

"Oh, yeah, you've never been here before. You can eat in there." She pointed toward a small dining-room area. I placed my food on the table and went in for the kill. Ten minutes later, Dahlia walked in, dressed in some of the shortest shorts I had ever seen her in. Her ass cheeks were almost out of the bottom on them. I was glad she wore a bra under the small white T she had on. I had to purposely make myself look away. She sat at the other end of the table and started to eat her burger. We fell silent for what seemed like an eternity.

"That was good," I burped and started to pat my stomach. I saw Dahlia roll her eyes in disgust. "What? A man can't burp?"

"I'm still eating. You could have covered your wolf breath." She started to laugh so hard that tears began to form in her eyes.

Her eyes are gorgeous. I hadn't noticed her eyes were a soft brown with a hint of grey in them. Maybe because I stopped looking Dahlia in the eyes years ago.

"Dang, Dahlia, talking about me sure makes you happy." I tried to sound like I was hurt. That didn't seem to faze her one bit. She had one of the prettiest smiles. It was weird because for the past two years all I've ever seen her do was frown, maybe because she hated me. *Maybe she doesn't hate me any more.*

"Aw, did I hurt your feelings? Well, too bad," she laughed again.

"Dahlia, one day you're going to stop being rude to me. I mean, I did see you naked today." Her smile disappeared and a look of embarrassment covered her face.

"You saw me naked?"

"No, don't get embarrassed. It was nice," I smirked.

She sucked in her teeth and said, "Ugh, don't go there, Mr. Washington. I don't go for the okeydoke."

I held up my hands in surrender. "Fine. I'll stop complimenting you."

The room fell silent again. I had been done with my food, but for some reason, I didn't have the urge to leave just yet. I know I was playing with fire by trying to attempt to flirt with the woman I couldn't stand for all this time. Not to mention she was Nitrah's best friend.

"Troy, what's going on here?"

Her expression showed she was serious and also confused. Hell, so was I. Why was I interested in her all of a sudden? "I don't know. I'm confused myself."

"What is it that you're confused about? What is this?"

I leaned forward and sighed. I should have just left after I was done eating. Why start something up with her? This could totally ruin any relationship I would ever have with Nitrah. I needed to stop. "It's weird, and I don't know how else to say it. I've seen a different side of you these past couple of days."

"Like what?"

"Funny, cute, a woman. Hell, you've made me laugh more times in the past two days then what I've done all year."

"Troy, OK, you should stop talking now. I don't want you to say or do something we both will regret." I could tell she had lost her appetite.

"I'm sorry, Dahlia." I stood up from the table and walked over and tossed my trash in her can. Then I turned back around and looked in her direction. "Don't you feel different toward me too?"

She mumbled something and said, "This can never happen, even if I wanted to go there. Maybe you're vulnerable. But what would happen if I said, 'Troy, I wish it was me and not Nitrah. That I never stopped loving you. That Robert was a clouded misjudgment'?"

"I'll say that I would have had to go through that with Nitrah to see that I still had some unfinished business with you."

She sighed out loud in frustration, placing her face in the palm of her hands. "Troy, forget everything I just said."

I leaned up against her wall and said, "Do you want me to leave?"

"I think it's best. Maybe we should just think about what we said here and let it sink in."

I walked over to her and knelt down and kissed her forehead. I didn't miss the fact that her eyes stayed glued to mine in the process. Her face was out of this world beautiful. *What the hell is going on here?*

"I'll see you some other time then. Take care, Dahlia." I grabbed my keys and walked out the door. I held my head low in shame. I couldn't go there. No matter my attraction to

Dahlia, I couldn't risk hurting Nitrah and never ever getting my family back. Or was Nitrah really worth it?

MAXWELL WAYNE

May 2005

The layout of Maxwell Too was like something out of a dream. I had just had a meeting with my architect and was on cloud nine with the final layouts she had agreed on. My dream was six months away from being a reality. I wanted to call up the guys and celebrate. I walked into Bar Eleven and noticed my brother Nick, and my best friend Gary, were seated at the bar a drink ahead of me.

"Yo', fellas, good to see you," I said, giving them a one-hand embrace.

"I ordered you a Crown and Coke," Gary said.

"Cool, I need this, y'all. The shit is about to come to life."

"Oh yeah, so how did it go today?" Nick asked.

"The layout was on point, and the workers are on time with their shit. Maxwell Too will be in business in six months. They'll be done building in four."

"I can't wait to manage it. The business is beginning to thrive, and you know since you have been off playing the daddy and shit I have been keeping tabs on everything," Gary added.

I grunted and said, "Gary, don't start with the Jazz jokes again."

"I'm just saying."

"I like Jazz. She's young, cute, a banging body, and now owns her own shit," Nick added.

"Thanks, bro." I knocked my glass against his.

"Oh, man, guess who came by the restaurant the other day?" Gary quizzed.

"I give up," I shrugged.

"Rayne." Suddenly my mood changed from excited to irritated.

"Rayne, your former fiancée Rayne? When did she get back?" Nick asked.

"A few months ago, and she came by the construction site. I don't want anything to do with that woman."

"She is fine as hell now. She's got a banging body."

"Gary, can you get off of every female's ass. Rayne ain't marriage material, and I'm done with her. I don't see why she won't get that through her head."

"So you *have* seen Rayne," Nick said.

"Nothing to worry about, bro. I gave her the walking papers. I'm just surprised she showed up again."

"You watch her, Maxwell. That bitch is evil, and when she hears about Jazz, I know she is going to cut loose."

"Bro, I'm certain she knows about Jazz by now."

I pulled up and noticed Tim's truck parked alongside the house. I sighed in frustration. I just wanted to come home to a quiet evening with my family. Yeah, Tim Jr. wasn't mine, but I was raising him like he was. But I just wish there wasn't a Tim Sr., the ex-husband, to have to see and deal with on a weekly basis. This is why Gary thought my relationship was a laughing matter. He despises women who already had babies. But Jazz wasn't just any woman. I believed God made her just for me.

I hopped out of the truck, pulling my dreads back to let some of the spring breeze run through them. I had sweated all day, and I was ready to lay it down. When I pushed open the front door, Tim's laughter greeted me. I rolled my eyes in annoyance. He thought he was slick by trying to be friendly and be in my woman's face all the time.

I would be lying if I didn't feel threatened by him. He stood over six feet, not a roll of fat on him. But he couldn't beat me when it came to looks. I know it sounds high schoolish, but hell, I had to stay on my p's and q's. I walked into the living area and noticed Junior had his travel backpack on.

"Hey, little man, you leaving?"

"Max," he yelled out in his tiny voice. Although he wasn't quite two years old yet, he had the speech of a four-year-old. He was smart, and I liked to think I had something to do with that.

"Hey, baby. Junior is going with Tim to New Orleans for the weekend. Their family is doing this reunion, and, of course, Tim wants to show him off," Jazz yelled loud enough for Tim to hear.

"Sho' 'nuff. That's my dude," Tim said, scooping Junior into his arms and giving me a one-hand shake. "All right, man, I'll see you and Jazz on Monday."

"All right, take care of our little man," I said to him as they walked out.

"So, babe, we have all this weekend to ourselves. What you want to do?" Jazz said, jumping up into my arms and wrapping her legs around my waist.

"Ummm, first, I'm going to do you, and then we'll think of something." I walked up toward the wall, pushing Jazz's body up against it.

"OOOOH, Max, you know this is one of my favorite positions." She ran her fingers through my dreads and kissed my lips. I was addicted to the way she looked at me.

I pushed her skirt up over her ass, feeling the thong that was in my way of gaining access to my favorite spot to be in. "Baby, you going to let me inside of you?" I whispered in between kisses.

"Yes, baby, I want to feel you in me now." Our kisses deepened as we hungrily breathed into each other's mouths, overcome with so much passion. By then, I had ripped her thong from her as she took her hands down to my belt and started to unbuckle it.

Then she pushed my pants down, bringing them to my calves. "Come on, baby, I want you to feel me."

I took one big thrust and threw myself inside of her. Her hot, slippery tunnel sucked me in deep as she tightened her walls around my dick. I could feel her tighten and then loosen her walls, just to do it all over again. I loved when she played with my dick like that. I took the palms of my hands and grabbed her cheeks, pulling them apart and using them to keep my balance. I pushed her harder up against the wall, bringing one of my legs forward so my dick could go in deeper. By then, I started to tremble at the sensation of feeling her around me raw. I buried my face in her neck as she squeezed my neck harder with each passing minute. I couldn't take the feeling anymore as my body weakened.

"Baby, I can't hold it."

"I'm about to come, baby, hold on," Jazz screamed out. When I heard her exhale, alerting me that she had fulfilled her desire, I pulled out and allowed my seed to explode in my hand.

Jazz slid down to the floor, breathing a mile a minute. "Now *that's* a welcome home." She laughed as I sprinted to the kitchen to fetch a napkin.

NITRAH HILL

The Lyrical Lounge was filled from wall to wall, and there was a waiting list to get in. I had one of the local popular poets hosting Soulful Fridays, which was the night I hosted Spoken Word and poetry readings. Along with a live jazz band playing, I created one of the best romantic atmospheres in the city of Fort Worth, Texas. I wasn't that type of owner who just sat in the back and watched other people work. I had on my apron, and at this very moment, I was in the kitchen calling orders, decorating the food, and making sure plates got out in time. I knew Jazz would be over to help in a minute. She was wrapping up a book signing with a local author in collaboration with tonight's event.

"Ms. Hill, the order is up," one of my cooks yelled. I took off my apron and picked up the tray, noticing one of my servers was MIA. I walked out and had to squeeze through the crowd as attendees tried to greet me and say hello.

"Hey, lady, let me go deliver this order. I'll be back," I said, in between brief hugs and kisses on the cheek. After dropping off the plates, I went by the bar and told Tony, my bartender, to get me a bottle of water. I was tired and decided to take a break and just enjoy the vibe of the place. That's when I noticed Jazz walk in with a few gift bags in tow and handed them to the first few guests she saw.

"Hey, lady. I just closed up shop next door. It's packed in here."

"Yes, ma'am. I just got through slaving in the kitchen. Damn me for adding on a food menu," I joked.

"Is Charmaine dropping through? I haven't heard from her this week."

"Supposed to. She's been working hard at the Social Security office. She said she needed the overtime." Jazz turned around to order a drink. "Hey, Tony, pass me a daiquiri, will you?"

"Hey, Jazz, what kind you want?" Tony called out.

"Strawberry, and you know it," she laughed.

"I see your boy Michael is here." She pointed toward the front door.

I hopped off my barstool. "Ooooh, he made it. I haven't seen him since he got kicked out of your and Maxwell's house last year. I need to get laid."

Rolling her eyes and laughing, she said, "Go do your thing, miss lady."

I hurried and walked over toward Michael's handsome self. He stood about 5'9' and always wore designer suits. His caramel skin and perfectly shaped gold T matched his million-dollar pearly smile, and just looking at him made me moist. And I needed to get laid. I hadn't had sex since Denim.

"Hey, Nini, you looking good, babe."

I knew he was lying. I felt hot, sweaty, and overworked. "You lie so well, Michael." I took my arms and wrapped them around his waist, giving him a tight squeeze. *Would it be wrong to ask him for sex after almost a year?*

I grabbed his hand and led him outside the balcony where a saxophonist was playing. From time to time, I had outside entertainment for the guests who had to sit on the outside balcony.

"Nini, your spot is looking real successful."

"Thanks to you," I said, taking a seat at my reserved table.

"I'm sorry I haven't been in town to see you. My move to California has had me occupied."

"I hate that you've moved so far away." I wasn't lying. Somehow, I had hoped for us to pick up where we left off.

"Yeah, me too, but work calls."

I pulled one of my servers to the side and ordered an appetizer.

"Michael, I'm glad you came to see me. I really do miss you, and I do have regrets about letting you go," I said, being honest and getting straight to the point. I noticed his demeanor change.

"Well, we all make decisions, Nini, but we got to learn to deal with them." That wasn't the reply I was looking for.

"I have doubts about the decision I made, and I wouldn't be lying if I said I didn't miss you."

"Nini, I thought you brought me out here just for a drink, not a trip down memory lane." I was surprised it looked like he had an attitude with me.

"I did, but we are together face-to-face for once. Why not tell you how I feel?"

"Maybe I don't care to know. Look, Nini, I thought we were friends. I have come to cope with that. But I am not interested going back and forth with you."

"I am not trying to go back and forth, Michael. I am trying to be honest. I made a mistake."

"No, you made your choice." He set his drink down and pushed his chair back.

"Wait—where are you going?"

"I see you had an alternative motive to inviting me here. I love you, Nitrah, but that you-and-I ship has sailed long ago when you chose Troy over me. Now what? Because you and Troy aren't together, it's 'let's go back to Michael then, the safe choice'?"

"No, it's not like that."

He threw up his hand and stood up. "Sure it is, Nitrah." I kept cringing at the fact that he was calling me Nitrah and not Nini. *I can not be losing Michael too.*

I reached for his arm in hopes of him sitting back down, but he dodged my reach. "Michael, I'm sorry if I seem like I don't know what I want. Maybe I didn't, but I did make a mistake. I do love you."

"Nitrah, I have to go. Take care of yourself."

"Wait," I called out. But he just kept walking. I couldn't make a scene in front of my guests. I had a reputation to keep. I held my head low and fought the tears that threatened to spring to life. Finally, I stood up and put my "A" game back on, walking back into the lounge. Immediately, I noticed Jazz and Charmaine were seated at the bar when I approached it.

Charmaine said, "Hey, Nitrah, you know I couldn't miss your Friday nights here." I gave her a gentle hug and thanked her for coming out. I was more than ready to go home. But go home to what? An empty house and a baby to raise? *Will I ever find someone to love me?*

JAZZARAY MEADOWS

You know that feeling when you know someone is watching you, but you don't know where and from what direction? This wasn't one of those moments because I knew who was "mean mugging" me, as they called it. A person who made sure I saw that she was watching me. I had been through enough in my life from being attacked by my ex-boyfriend and accidently killing him that I felt that if it came down to it, I could fight a bitch off. So I was mentally preparing myself to fight this heifa who was in my store. She was drinking up my cappuccino and acting like she was reading a book. I knew damn well she was more interested in eyeballing me, though. *I'm about two seconds away from kicking her butt out.*

I didn't know her nor had I seen her before, so I didn't know what the issue was. "Jazz, do you know that woman?" one of my employees asked.

"No, but prepare to back me up if shit hits the fan. I'm about to approach her." I didn't wait for her to reply as I made my way to the mysterious woman's table.

"Jazz, isn't it?" the stranger said before I could finish my walk over.

"Who's asking?"

She extended her hand and said, “I’m Rayne.” I left her hand hanging. I wasn’t too keen on acting like I liked someone. And I didn’t like her already. She dropped her hand back into her lap.

“Rayne?”

“Yes. We don’t know each other, but I am an old friend of the family. Of Mr. Wayne’s family, that is.”

I raised an eyebrow. *Oh, so she is a former jump-off of Max’s.* I started to smirk because I figured she thought I should be intimidated by her.

“What’s so funny?”

“So you and Maxwell use to be together, huh? And now you sitting in my bookstore telling me this information because …?” I folded my arms and tapped my foot, showing her that I was not moved by her little show.

Stuttering, she said, “Well, since you’re so straight-up, let me get to the point.”

“Please do, because I do have shit to do today.”

“I’m back, and I want Maxwell, and that cannot be easily done with you in the way.”

Blowing out hot air I said, “And you tell me this information because …? Look, Ms. Rayne. Tell Maxwell about your little plan, okay? I don’t give a shit what you got planned. A man will go where he damn well pleases, and I have learned that simple bitches like you are a waste of breath. I don’t care about you sitting in here threatening me that you back in town. Who cares? Sweetheart, I am not a gullible female. Take that mess to someone else." I popped my neck and rolled my eyes, proud of the speech I gave her.

"I see Maxwell went and got him a ghetto bitch."

My employee walked up behind me and said, "Ma'am, I think it's time that you leave. And do not return. You aren't welcomed back." I watched her pick up her purse and smack her lips at me.

"Jazz, I know she pissed you off but please act civilized in your place of business." I stared my employee down but couldn't say anything because she was right. I nodded my head and went back to my office where I picked up the phone and called Max.

"Hey, baby, you must not be busy to be calling me during the day."

"Rayne is why I'm calling."

"Did you say Rayne?"

"Yep."

"Why? Was she there?"

"Yep."

"Did you speak to her?"

"Yep."

"Jazz, baby, give me more than just a yep."

"She plans to take you away from me," I laughed.

"I'm sorry I didn't tell you about her, Jazz, baby. But just out of the blue she has been popping up everywhere."

"That sounds like stalking, Max, not popping up."

"No, I don't think she will go that far."

"Hello! I just said she was in *my* store. Sat here for thirty minutes mean mugging me."

"I'll talk to her."

"I'm so sure you will, Max."

"All I'm going to do is talk to her, Jazz." I started to envision him and Rayne talking in a dark room, in one her well-planned traps. She would turn her double D breasts toward Max, and from that point on, he would be hypnotized by her. Fucking is what they were going to end up doing. But I had to trust Max. I knew he was finer than wine, and I couldn't let my insecurities get the best of me.

"I believe you, Max. I'll see you tonight at home."

"I love you, Jazz, baby."

"Love you too."

It was well after three and the store was slow. I decided to let my manager take over for the rest of the day and drive out to see Dahlia. I had promised her lunch several weeks ago, and I knew by the time I made it out to Irving, she should be ready to go and grab some food. I walked out and glanced over toward the lounge and noticed Nitrah's car out front. She was in later than usual. Normally, she would have left by now for a midday break to go get Nina. I decided to just hop in the car and talk to her later.

I smiled at the new SUV Max got me and hopped my little self into the driver's seat, pushed it forward to reach the peddle, and drove off, headed on Highway 30. An hour later after fighting with traffic, I pulled up in front of Dahlia's office building. The parking lot was only half full, meaning the top execs she worked for were leaving.

I turned off my engine and grabbed my purse from the floor of my car. Unbuckling my seat belt, I reached down further, struggling to find exactly where I threw my phone earlier. I felt its cold metal touch my hand and grabbed it, throwing myself back up into the driver's seat. Quickly, I punched in Dahlia's number and leaned back, watching the corporate workers go in and out of the building.

Three rings went by, and then voice mail. "Oh no, she didn't send me to voice mail." I proceeded to punch her number back into my phone when I glanced up and saw a familiar face. "What is Troy doing here?"

I started to lower my window and yell his name when I saw Dahlia run out of the office holding a bag up toward Troy. He turned around and laughed, obviously stating that he had forgotten it. He leaned down and gave her a hug and kissed her forehead.

"Wait a minute now. These two can't stand each other. What the hell is this?" Dahlia looked up at him and smiled. I had never seen her in the almost four years of knowing Troy look at him like that. *She likes him.* "Oh my God, they are fucking!" I screamed out. Embarrassed, I had to look around the cars to see if anyone heard me.

My rage started to boil over as I watched them interact with each other. He was brushing her curls behind her ear, and her hand was placed on his waist. I could not believe what I was watching. This *cannot* be happening. "NO, NO, NO!" I didn't notice the furious tears that stung my eyes until my vision became blurry.

"Why would Dahlia and Troy do this? I thought Dahlia was our friend," I said to myself. Not able to take any more of this crap, I placed my SUV in reverse and nervously pulled out of the parking lot. My hands were shaking as I tried to control the wheel. I didn't know what to do with what I had just seen. Troy wasn't my man, but I knew I was going to witness hell when the shit hit the fan.

TROY WASHINGTON

It was a week later after my initial encounter with Dahlia that I was standing on her front porch ringing her doorbell. Something told me to turn around, to just walk away. That's didn't happen. Something was drawing me to this woman. The woman who I couldn't stand for the most part, but the woman I remember from back in college has been taking the front seat. She wasn't a bad girlfriend at all back then. But the only reason why I was so-called dating her is because my frat brothers assigned me to her.

I was one of the ten pledges at Prairie View A&M, and along with the many embarrassing things they made us do, we had to find an easy woman who we would have to film having sex with. I wanted to be a KAPPA so bad that I agreed to do it. Getting a woman wasn't hard for me anyhow. I had a different woman in my bed every night. But they decided that my task had to be hard, and Dahlia was what they called a good girl. She wouldn't give it up to anyone, and it was my job to break her down. Long story short, I did sleep with her, but in the process of hurting her, I was too embarrassed to take the KAPPA's brotherhood. I transferred schools a little after that, afraid that the dean would find out, and then my mother. I would never want my mother to find out some of the things I used to do.

Four years passed before I saw her again, and this time, she had Nitrah with her. Nitrah was who I wanted. She had a cockiness about her, and her dark skin had a cream look to it that made her look almost untouchable. Her smile had made me hard on the spot. But after dating Nitrah for almost a year, I found out that she dated me as a ploy for Dahlia's revenge. That took away everything we could have possibly been together.

I still loved Nitrah, but I wasn't sure about being in love with her anymore. The odd thing about it was I didn't feel guilty about changing up and wanting to pursue Dahlia. I mean, I did date her first, and we did have unfinished business.

Dahlia peeked her head out of the door and said, "Troy, what are you doing here?"

"That's right, I didn't call first," I said.

"Of course, you didn't call, because if you had, I would have told you to not come," she said.

"Why, Dahlia?"

"Troy, what is it that you want from me?"

"I honestly am blindsided by the way I feel about you. Should we even go there I don't know yet. But I do know that we have some unfinished business. Just let me take you out. If nothing happens, nothing happens."

She bit her bottom lip and started to think about my proposition. "If nothing happens do you promise to stop stalking me?"

I laughed and said, "Yes, Dahlia, I'll stop pursuing you."

She widened her door to let me in and said, "So you're pursuing me?"

I walked in and plopped down on her couch and said, "Just go put something on, woman, and stop asking me questions."

She smirked and walked back to her room. My eyes followed her ass, and my dick hardened. *Damn, what am I going to do about you?* I looked down at my pants and tried to rearrange the imprint it was making in my jeans.

I swear women take forever to get ready. I yelled for Dahlia to hurry up five times before she made her way out to the living room.

"Is this OK for where you're taking me?" She twirled around in a tight-fitted black dress that barely covered her ass and thighs. I don't know why I hadn't noticed that Dahlia was built like a brick house until just now. She had more than a handful of ass and breasts.

"You look a'ight," I lied. "Let's go now." She blew out air and rolled her eyes at my reply. I had to hide my laughter.

We arrived in Hurst, a small city outside of Fort Worth, at a restaurant called Cheddar's. They had some of the best nachos in the area. The hostess sat us at a booth near the rear of the store. I had a feeling Dahlia was excited about us sitting in the back.

"So, Troy, you got me here. Now woo me."

"In due time," I boasted.

We grew quiet for about five minutes. I guess we both were lost in the trance. *What are we doing here? Why did we like each other? Will we go any further?* I'm sure she asked herself these same questions as did I.

"Troy, have you thought about the consequences to our actions?"

"Like who will be hurt?"

"Yes. Believe it or not, Nitrah and you are connected for life. You have Nina. You and I together will only complicate things. She's my best friend."

"I know, Dahlia. This I do know. But I can't get over the fact that I was with you first."

"Are we taking it back there now?"

"What?"

"To college. I know you *don't* want to take it there."

"I don't want to remember the night I hurt you. I just want to remember the good parts."

"What if we date, and it still doesn't work out? We would lose all of our friends for nothing."

"What if it did work out?"

"My girls would never forgive me."

"They forgave Nitrah. You forgave her."

"That was different."

"How, Dahlia? How was Nitrah and I being together different?"

"I don't know; it just was."

"It may be different because everyone accepted Nitrah and me. They may do the same for us."

"What about your brother?"

"What about Robert?"

"I dated him. We were in love. How would he feel about us together again?"

"The same way I felt when you dated my brother."

"That was different."

The table grew quiet, and then we both burst out into laughter. "See, Dahlia, we have both done some shit. But it won't matter."

"Troy, I stopped loving you years ago."

"Did you, Dahlia, or did you just accept the fact that I was with Nitrah?"

I could tell she was lost in her thoughts thinking about the question in her head.

"Troy, maybe a little of both."

"But …?"

"But what good is our happiness if it destroys everyone else's. Those girls are my life. I have no other friends."

"What if we sat down together at some point, once we understand what is going on between us? I don't want to hurt Nitrah, but we have to follow our hearts, right?"

"Do we?"

"I don't want to go through life wondering."

"Neither do I."

"Well, then, it's official. You are my undercover freak … I mean, girl." I laughed.

She threw her napkin at me and leaned back in her seat clearly exhaling. "I'm going to trust you, Troy, and follow your lead."

We ordered our food and sat and caught up with each other's lives over the past few years. It was funny how our lives overlapped with knowing the same people, but we never took the time to just talk. It was nice talking to her and to see her smile. I told her she should smile more often.

She said, "I think you've given me a reason to."

I had my face buried in the pillow as he pounded in and out of me. It felt good in the beginning, but after a while, I started to feel like he forgot I was there. He demanded that I open my legs wider, and I obeyed, holding back the agony that was stuck in my throat. I couldn't wait for him to finish.

Finally, I could feel his grip loosen as his satisfaction was reaching its climax. At last, I became limp and threw myself across my bed. My vagina was still pounding and burning.

"That's all you came over to do, Tim?"

"Damn, Char, give me a minute before you start bitching," he said, grabbing a towel and wiping off his private area.

"I'm just saying I haven't heard from you all month. Your whores keeping you busy, I see."

"Ugh, there you go again. I didn't come over to fuck you and hear this shit. That's what you wanted, right? A good fuck."

"Yeah, hint: word *good*."

"Whatever. I got to head back over to the construction site."

I became nervous as I started to prepare myself to ask him for what I really wanted. "Tim!"

"Yeah?" he said, throwing mouthwash into his mouth.

"I need a favor, please."

He walked out of the bathroom, pulling up his pants. "What is it?"

"I'm a little low on cash. Can you please spare me something?"

"How the hell you low on cash? You're the director now at the Social Security office."

"Yeah, and Joy knows that too."

"Joy who?"

"Joyclyn."

He grunted and said, "What that bitch want now? She still blackmailing you?"

"Yeah, and only me for some reason. I don't know why it ain't the both of us."

"I hate that bitch. I should go see her and beat her ass," Tim yelled.

"Can you just give me some money instead?"

"Why the fuck you paying her anyhow?"

"Because I'm trying to keep us a secret."

"Why haven't you used the fact that she fucked Bobby in your house? You haven't even told her friends that, and it's been six months."

"Tim, can you just please give me some money? I'll handle things."

He reached for his wallet and pulled out four twenties. "Here, and if Joyclyn come asking for more money, tell her I will come pay her a visit."

"Sure, Tim, whatever you say. But if she runs off and tells Jazz about us, what then?"

He blew out hot air and started to rub his temples. "We got to get that ho out of Fort Worth and soon. I'm not trying to knock the chance to get back with Jazz. I know that nigga she with ain't only fucking her, and when she realize it, she'll be right back with me."

"Whatever, Tim. Thanks for the money."

He grabbed his shirt and walked out of the house. I knew Tim was adamant about not paying off Joyclyn, but if she ever opened her mouth about what she knew, our lives as we knew it would be over.

DENIM OVERTON

Club Taste was on point tonight. I hadn't been home since before last Thanksgiving and the crowd was showing me love. I had just debuted a new song by one of my up-and-coming artists and the response was crazy. The best thing about it was my best friend Dalvin was here. I hadn't seen him in a couple of years. We used to be everywhere together before I started producing and moved to Houston a couple years back. He was recently divorced and ready to tag team some of these groupies along with me.

"Yo', you see that young one over there." He pointed toward the crowd.

"Hey D, be careful with the young ones. Most of them are lying about their age. Go with the ones you know are over 25." I wasn't joking either.

He took another swallow of his liquor and said he was about to go find somebody to dance with. I laughed at him and watched him walk in the crowd. He was never the type to approach a woman for whatever reason. So I watched him try to act like me.

"It's good to see you two are still friends."

I turned around to see who was acting like they knew me when a familiar face stood before me. "Well, I be damned. If it ain't Sarah."

"Oh, so you remember me."

I leaned in and gave her a hug and said, "How can I forget you broke my heart?" I teased.

"I think it was the other way around," she smiled. I was surprised to see her smiling at me since our relationship didn't end so good. It was over two years ago when Sarah and I dated. It ended because she felt I was still in love with Nitrah. Which I was, but in the end, I ended up in bed with Sarah's friend Kia.

"I was just thinking about how we broke up."

"Oh yeah, and what did you conclude?" she asked.

"That I fucked up, and let me just say, I apologize right now." I placed my hand over my heart and pretended I was heartbroken. She laughed and waved me off.

"It's cool, Denim. You sleeping with Kia helped me find myself and my current husband." She flashed her ring toward me. It was pretty sizeable too. That was a slap in the face. I expected her to flirt or act like she wanted to rekindle something. I mean, after all, I was DJ Denim O, worth over twenty million.

"Married, huh? Well, congrats."

"Thank you, and how about yourself?" Just then, like clockwork, I saw Nitrah walk in the club toward the bar. I hadn't really made up with her since our fight a few months back, but now was no better time to show Sarah that I was still with the woman that she hated so much.

"Here comes my baby now. Yo', Nitrah! Over here!" I saw Sarah raise her eyebrow in a curious but jealous way, and I felt satisfied with her reaction.

"Hey, Denim, why are you yelling all across the club like that?"

I pulled Nitrah into my arms and swung her around to face Sarah. "Nitrah, you remembers Sarah, right?

"Sarah, Nitrah!"

I could hear the hesitation in Nitrah's voice as she extended her hand. "Hey, Sarah, it's been a very long time." I knew Nitrah didn't like Sarah. She was the very reason why Nitrah and I broke up and why Nitrah hooked up with Troy in the first place.

Sarah took her hand and said, "Yes, a very long time. I'm happy to see you two together still."

"Together?" Nitrah quizzed.

I cut her off and said, "Yeah, it's been hard with the transformation of my life, but we make it work."

Nitrah turned and eyeballed me.

"Well, I'm going to get a drink and leave you two alone. Oh, and congrats on the success, Denim, and best of luck." I nodded my head and said thank you as she walked away.

Nitrah swung around and placed her hands on her hip. "Fronting in front of your ex? DJ Denim O still has to pretend, huh?"

"Nitrah, don't give me much grief, a'ight? I'll tell you about why I did that later. Right now, I'm in town. I haven't seen you in some months, and I want to just wild out. Okay?"

"Fine, Denim, whatever you say." She rolled her eyes and looked toward the bartender to make her a drink.

I stayed at the club for what seemed like an eternity, but what only turned out to be one o'clock in the morning. Shocked that I was tired so early, I rubbed my eyes and told my assistant to get the driver. I was ready to go.

"Nitrah, ride with me. I'll have my assistant drive behind us in your car, cool?"

"You tired already?"

"Yeah, I just want to go back to the room and lay my head on your stomach and go to sleep."

"I didn't volunteer to be your pillow tonight," she laughed.

"Come on." I grabbed her hand and told the crew I was gone for the night. I said good-bye to a few of the promoters and hopped in the back of my rented hummer with Nitrah. Dalvin decided to stay with a few of the groupies who decided to stick with him because they couldn't get to me. I happily obliged.

It didn't take long for me to fall into a deep sleep. I opened my eyes to my driver opening my door and announcing that we had arrived at the Hilton. Then I tapped Nitrah's leg to wake her up, and she followed me into the lobby.

Once upstairs, I gave my bodyguard the okay to leave for the night and walked Nitrah inside of my suite.

"This is nice as usual," she said pulling her shoes off and tossing them to the floor. She slid out of her pants, and all I could see was her half-cut black panties that allowed her apple cheeks to hang below.

I reached over to the satellite radio and turned on some jazz. Then I stripped out of my clothes and walked over and plopped down on the bed. Nitrah started to squirm and giggle under the sheets, remarking about how soft they were.

I started to get excited myself, knowing that this sleep I was about to tackle was about to be really good. I reached over and pulled Nitrah's body closer to mine and placed my head on her stomach. Then I was out like a light.

I woke up with Denim's heavy head on my abdomen. Gently, I pushed him to the side so that I could turn over and get comfortable. Soon, I started to hear a buzzing noise and noticed it was my phone ringing. I had it on vibrate. Quietly, I tiptoed over to my purse and located my phone and flipped it open.

"Hello," I whispered.

"Hey, are you up yet?" I heard Troy's voice come through the phone. I located a table clock that read 6:00 a.m. I instantly became annoyed at this early phone call. I walked over to the balcony and slid open the door and walked out to the morning breeze. The sun wasn't quite all the way up just yet.

"I'm up now. What's wrong? Is something wrong with Nina?"

"No, I couldn't sleep."

Annoyed, I breathed out and sat down on the bench, pulling my knees to my chest. "OK, you couldn't sleep and what?"

"I knew no one else would answer the phone, so I'm calling to bug you." This was a change of events. I hadn't held too many conversations with Troy in months, only to say hi and bye and to simply make arrangements for him to get Nina.

"So you decided to call me. I'm not quite your best friend in the world, so what's up?"

"Yeah, I'm trying to understand why we can't even hold a conversation with each other. I'm trying to be civil."

"At six in the morning, Troy? You could have waited till at least eight or nine," I yawned.

"You wanna talk or what?" he quizzed.

"OK, Mr. Washington, talk; I'm listening," I teased.

"I just got this thought, you know. I've been tripping lately. Been having some thoughts I'm not supposed to have, and then I remembered I'm supposed to be changing, you know."

"Changing to what?"

"Into a good man for you and Nina. But how can I do that if all I did was leave? We never talked."

"True, but we knew this was coming. You held a grudge against me, and there wasn't much I could do. I couldn't turn back the hands of time."

"You're right, but in the end, you still tried to make it work. I can't move on until I know that this chapter is closed."

"So this is why you call me so early in the morning?"

"Yeah, part of it. I also need to see you."

"You see me every week, Troy."

"No, not just to drop off Nina. I need to spend time with you before I make any huge decisions that can change us."

"OK, what is really going on? What decisions?"

"Don't worry about that for now. Just say you'll go out with me."

"I guess if you say so. Where to and when?"

"I'm going to have Nina stay with Mama tonight. I'll come and pick you up from the house."

"Does it have to be tonight? I have friends in from out of town."

"Who, Denim?"

"Well, yeah. I haven't seen him since Thanksgiving, and he's in town for a show, and he was going to … never mind. I'll see you tonight." I figured I shouldn't say much about Denim to Troy.

"I know he's your friend. How about tomorrow night then?"

That was different. Troy didn't argue with me about Denim. "OK, that's perfect. I'll be over to get Nina for a bit from your mother's. We're going to take her to the zoo, okay?"

"That's fine. Love you, Nitrah."

I glanced at the phone to make sure I heard him right. "Huh?"

"I know, weird, huh? But I do. I'll talk to you later." Then he hung up. He hadn't said I love you since before he moved out. *What is really going on?*

I walked back into the hotel room to see Denim still in a deep sleep. It was now 6:30 a.m. and with only four hours of sleep, I slipped back onto my side of the bed and decided to get a couple more hours of sleep.

It was Denim's younger cousin's high school graduation dinner at Denim's mom's house and everyone I knew or used to know was in attendance. Denim's mom hugged me so tightly that I ached when I breathed in afterward. "There's my daughter-in-law," she said out loud for everyone to hear. I blushed and went with the flow. I had known the Overton family since I was in grade school. Their aunts were my aunts; their cousins were my cousins; and Denim's sisters were my sisters.

I was excited to see both of my sisters, Raven and Tierra, in town, and they came over with my parents to enjoy the BBQ. Denim's dad had on his chef apron and was in the backyard cooking up some chicken, baloney, sausage, ribs, brisket, and hot dogs. I decided to help Denim's mom with the potato salad. She was teaching me how to cook it.

"OK, Miss Thang, grab a few of those eggs and pass me the relish," she said. I obeyed orders and pretended I was listening to her instructions, but I was distracted by a familiar face in the crowd. I knew him, but I didn't know him. I was curious to know who he was. I managed to sneak out of the kitchen and into the bathroom to wash my hands when I heard a tap on the door.

When I swung open the door, lo and behold, Mr. Mystery Man was standing there. "Hi," I said.

"Oh, I didn't know anyone was in here. I'll wait."

I reached for a napkin and proceeded to dry my hands, trying to not be obvious with my investigation of who this fine, tall, dark drink of chocolate was.

"I'm done," I said, sliding by. He looked directly into my face as we squeezed past each other in that tight doorway, my breasts brushing against his chest.

"Hope to see you later," he said, licking his lips. My vagina did a full 360-degree turn and grew tight at the sight of his lips. *Let me get away from this fine-ass man.* I didn't know who Mr. Mystery Man was and until I did, I had to stay clear. I didn't want a long-lost brother of Denim's to be barking up my tree, asking for some nookie.

I walked back into the living room and flopped down beside Tierra, my sister. "Do you know who that chocolate brother who looks like Idris Elba is?"

"Oh, I think that's Darrell's friend."

"Who's Darrell?"

"You know Sasha's best friend's brother." Sasha was Denim's older sister and her best friend who was an old college roommate. That meant one thing. The tall drink of chocolate wasn't any kin to Denim. My smile must have been obvious.

"Oh, that must be good news, huh?"

"What?" I bashfully said, trying to hide the obvious.

"You like him, and you were trying to see who he was and who he was with." Tierra started to laugh. I shushed her and looked down the hallway to see when Mr. Mystery Man was going to reappear. And he did two minutes later. He had the swagger of a thug, but the smile of a pretty boy.

"He's walking over here, Tierra," I whispered.

"Good. Let me leave so you can get your mack on." She jumped up off the couch before I could protest. I tried to look in the opposite direction, pretending I was engrossed in Nina making a mess of the cake Raven had given her.

"This seat taken?" he asked.

"Oh no, my sister left. You can sit here if you want." *Yeah, sit your fine ass right next to me. Where's Denim? I hope he ain't watching.*

"You don't remember me, do you? I used to go to school with your older sister Raven."

"Oh, really? No, I can't say that I do. I was a coming-in freshman by the time y'all graduated."

"Oh, yeah, but I remember you from here and there. I'm Marlo." He extended his hand for me to shake.

I raised a curious eyebrow and butterflies started to take off in my stomach. "Hey, Marlo, I'm Nitrah." I took his hand in mine.

"Yeah, I know. You also own that popular club, Lit something, right?" *He knows damn well what the name of my lounge is. He's trying to get personal, so let me play along.*

"Yeah, the Lyrical Lounge."

"Right. I've been meaning to go there. Seems everyone does already. Maybe now I have a reason to."

"Yeah, maybe you do," I flirted back.

"Hey, Nitrah, come here. Pops wants to show you something," I heard Denim yell over the crowd from outside.

"Well, Marlo, that's my cue to go, but hey, don't be a stranger."

"Trust, I won't."

I smiled and rose from the couch making sure to put a little more swing in my hips than usual.

MAXWELL WAYNE

It was well after two a.m. on a Saturday night, and I had decided to close up and let my staff go home. I walked around the empty restaurant and turned off individual lights on various tables. Then I lazily reached down and pulled off my shoes, toting them in my hands as I made my rounds.

After I was satisfied with the amount of lights turned off, I walked back to my office, pressing the security code in the pad. Quickly, I rushed to my office door, grabbed my suitcase, and rushed out the back exit before my thirty seconds was up and the alarmed sounded.

Pulling out my keys, I heard someone say, "Still ignoring me, huh?"

I breathed a sigh of agony as I realized Rayne was back. "What is it now?"

"Why haven't you even tried to talk to me, Maxwell, since I've been back home? It's been months."

I opened the back door to my truck and threw my suitcase in the seat. "Rayne, it's late, and I don't feel like it."

"Look, all I want to do is talk," she said, walking toward my truck and leaning up against it.

"It's well after two in the morning. I don't have time for this."

"Just give me one day. One date. Then I'll leave you alone."

"Rayne," I yelled.

"Just one and I'll leave you and little ole Jazz be."

"Fine, one date. Meet me around three at your place."

"Prefect." She leaned in toward me and kissed my check, making sure I felt her hardened nipples on my chest.

I dreaded going to go see Rayne, but I needed to talk to her alone and get her straightened out. I once loved this woman. I was 26 when I decided to pop the question to her and ask her to marry me, but now, being all of 32, I was more focused on the new woman in my life. That woman was Jazz. She didn't care about all the money I had. She loves me for who I am, and she doesn't interrogate me every time I walk into the house like Rayne used to do.

I used to wonder about all the what-ifs when it came to Rayne. What if she hadn't moved to D.C.? What if she was the mother to my children? What if this and what if that. I pulled up in front of her condo and walked up to her front door. Like I had imagined, she was watching me pull up and was already standing at the door.

"On time. Still the same ole Maxwell." I noticed the tight shirt she wore clearly displayed that she was braless. A woman with perfect breasts like Rayne should never go without a bra. It was just too tempting.

I grunted and slid past her and walked in. "I got five minutes for you, Rayne, and than I expect you to leave me alone for good."

"That's fine. I don't need any more time than that."

I walked over and plopped down on the couch, only to have been blindsided with Rayne's eager jump into my lap. She straddled her legs on both sides of me, firmly planting herself.

"I've so missed you," she mumbled, bringing her lips to my collarbone.

My instant reaction was to push her off me, but she had a grip like a lion out for its prey. Then I thought, *I am her prey.* She hurriedly took her hands and raised her shirt over her head, revealing her supple breasts.

I held up my hands, refusing to touch her like she wanted and said, "Rayne, stop. This is not what I came over here for."

"Come on, Maxwell, who am I going to tell?" She leaned in further, bringing her lips behind my ear, remembering that used to be my weak spot. I felt my dick harden on cue. *Shit, I got this get this woman off of me.*

I caught myself when I felt a soft moan escape my mouth.

"Yeah, baby, that's it. You like that, don't you. Do you miss us?"

I took a deep breath with my hands still raised in the air. "Rayne, I don't want to hurt you but get up now." My cry was weak, and she knew it. I was no stronger to walk away than a teenage boy sniffing the pussy for the first time.

I felt my hands slowly lower as I felt her hands trail down to the opening of my pants. She hopped off my lap and in record time, I looked down to see my exposed dick in her hand. She bent over and took me into her mouth, and instantly, my head fell back against the wall. The heat from her mouth caused me to extend my enlarged shaft to the depths of her mouth. I squeezed my eyes shut, not believing that I was allowing this to happen but too weak to tell her to stop.

I hadn't been in her house two minutes, and already, my dick was in her mouth. I raised my head when I felt Rayne's grip disappear from me. Opening my eyes, I noticed she had taken off her shorts and stood there naked.

"Rayne, enough is enough," I cried out. *Damn, what's wrong with me?* She leaned in toward me, brushing her breast across my lips, and I noticed my mouth open to allow a nipple to fall in. Unable to control myself, my mouth began to suck on her breast like I was eagerly searching for honey to sip out of it.

She straddled her legs around me again and slowly lowered herself on my shaft and started to ride. "Yes, Maxwell, fuck me, baby," I heard her call out. I could feel my hips gyrate in a rhythm with hers as her juices flowed.

Our speed heightened as the intensity of our sex began to overflow. I felt myself reach the max and placed my hands on her ass to move her rhythm harder and faster to completely enjoy my climax. Then my seed exploded inside her as our rhythm subsided.

"Get off me," I whispered with a dry mouth but with complete anger. I was angrier at myself for being weak to her. But then the thought of having unprotected sex with her started to race through my mind. I jumped up off the couch and zipped up my pants. "Rayne, I will kill you if you tell Jazz about this. Don't call me or come anywhere around me ever again, you got it?" I placed my hand hard around her neck to make sure that she knew I was dead serious.

She struggled and nodded her head yes. Then I pushed her down on the couch and walked out the door, slamming it hard behind me. By then, I started to panic because I knew that if Jazz found out, she would leave me.

It was only yesterday that I saw my best friend with my other best friend's boyfriend and baby's father. Now who was I to tell that this mess was going down? How was I supposed to look Dahlia in the face and not want to punch that face? She had called my phone twice, and I had to send her straight to voice mail. I knew that Nitrah was out with Denim because he was in town now. I could only think of one mutual friend to call and a former husband.

"Hey, Jazz, what's up?"

"Where are you? I need to speak to you about something."

"Running back to me already, I see. Let me finish up here at the construction site, and I'll meet in, oh, say, two hours," he joked.

"It ain't about you and me. Just meet me at Mama's house. You can pick me up a smoothie from Sonic while you're at it."

"OK, OK, OK, Jazz. I'll see you over there."

He was thirty minutes later than usual, but I didn't care. I had to get what I needed to say off my chest. I couldn't mention names just yet. But hey, he wasn't that dumb. He'll probably guess who I was talking about.

He walked up on the porch and sat down next to me in the empty chair, handing me my smoothie. "Thanks," I said, placing the straw in my mouth and taking a sip.

"OK, you got me here. Now what's up?"

"I witnessed something the other day, and I don't know how to just come out and say it."

"Just say it. No other way to," he said, leaning forward and placing his elbows on his knees.

"One of my best friends is betraying me and some of my other friends."

"Betraying you how?"

"The line you should never cross."

"And that is?"

I saw him getting impatient, so I cut straight to the chase. "She is sleeping with an ex that one of my friends used to date and even has a child with."

He jumped out of his seat. "What?"

I didn't expect him to get this hyper over news from me. "Yeah, and now I'm upset, hurt, crushed, and I don't know what to say to my friend," I eyed him.

"Jazz, I'm so sorry. I didn't mean for this to happen."

Raising my eyebrow, I said, "Huh? What are *you* apologizing for?"

He grew silent and started to stutter over his words. "I was just feeling your pain. I mean, it's horrible." I could tell he was lying even before he said the lie.

"Wait, Tim, why would *you* be apologizing as if you did something? Am I missing something?"

"Let's not get off track here, Jazz. How do you want me to help you in this situation?" Not trying to stress whatever the hell he was talking about, I went back to the story while remembering to bring up what he was lying about later.

"I wanted to know how I tell her."

"Tell who?"

"The best friend who is getting betrayed."

"You don't."

"What do you mean? I can't lie and see her get hurt."

"Jazz, women are crazy. They hate the messenger. If you want this to come out in the light, make it come out on its own."

"So I pretend I don't know?"

"No, you just keep quiet until the time is right. I honestly don't see anything good coming out of you saying anything. Just don't say anything."

"Ugh. I'm asking the wrong person. I'm talking to someone who has a different woman in his bed every night."

"Trust me, Jazz. And by the way, it's not every night." He laughed. I rolled my eyes in disgust.

"You used to be a good man, Tim. Now you're just back to your old ways. It was only a matter of time before you would have hurt me anyhow."

"Now, Jazz, how did we get there?"

"I'm just saying. You used to be different when you were with me."

"Well, you left me, remember? I don't have you any more, so there isn't a point to be that Tim any more." He grew quiet, and I looked at his face. It was a mixture of sadness and regret.

"Yeah, you can, and you got to live by example for Junior, you know?"

"Yeah, maybe I will when he gets older and grows a dick." I rolled my eyes and rose up from my chair.

"I'll keep quiet, but as for the backstabbing friend, I can't smile in her face, so I'm cutting her loose."

"How you gonna do that without her seeing a change in you?"

"I don't know."

"Who are these friends anyhow?"

"In due time, Tim, you'll know. Follow me to Denny's will you? I'm hungry."

"Fine, but you treating. I just gave away my last hundred today."

Denim was flying back out today so I started to prepare for my date with Troy. I dressed Nina in a new Care Bear outfit my sister had bought her and took her over to Jailen's, my brother's, house for the night. I didn't know what to expect from the night out with Troy, but I was hoping to possibly come to terms with our relationship. I loved him, but at the end of the day, if he couldn't forgive me for keeping Nina away from him for almost a year, then our relationship wouldn't last anyhow.

I pulled up to Jingles, a local dance spot that folks went to eat and dance at. I remember Jazz telling me that Maxwell and she had came here when they first met. Maybe this place would rekindle a romance I had with Troy like it had done with Maxwell. I was dressed seductive just to make a point. My dress hugged all of my curves, my breasts showed just the right amount of cleavage, and I was wearing Baby Phat perfume, the one that used to make Troy hard just from the smell of it.

We hadn't had sex in mouths, but I wouldn't mind climbing his pole tonight, just for old time's sake. He was never bad in bed anyhow. I walked in and allowed the hostess to walk me over to Troy's table. I showed up thirty minutes late on purpose just so he would have to watch me walk in. I didn't dress this fine for him to just see me sitting down in it. Turning the corner, it seemed everyone in the room disappeared and there he sat. *Damn, he is looking mighty fine. This is going to be harder than I thought.*

He stood up and leaned in toward me, kissing my cheek, "Hey, Nitrah, you looking good, woman."

"You are looking pretty good yourself." I trailed my hand down his arm after our brief embrace and felt his biceps contract. My inner loins jumped instantly. *Calm down, Nitrah.*

"So this is a nice spot. I haven't been here before," I continued.

"Yeah, I figured coming to a new spot would be good for us. Where did you drop off Nina tonight?"

"With Jailen. I think he's using Nina to woo some new girl of his," I added. Troy nodded his head and picked up the menu.

"Oh, I see they have chicken fried steak. I'm getting that," I said, with my mouth already watering. Troy began to laugh. "What's so funny?" I asked innocently.

"Nothing. I mean, why don't you get something different for a change? It's always chicken fried steak."

"Why? I bet you're going to get a steak anyhow. Your usual," I teased. He gave that *I'm busted* look.

"OK, you got me. Well, if I get a pasta dish, you get one with me too."

"Ugh, do I have to?" I whined. I liked this little game. He gave that *don't play with me look.* "Fine. I'll get the shrimp Alfredo."

"I'll get that too." He handed the server our menus and placed the order.

"So thank you for coming to meet me tonight."

"No problem," I said, leaning forward to pick up my water and take a sip.

"So catch me up with what's been going on with you."

"Troy, instead, can we talk about why you left?"

He sighed and started to look out the window we were seated next to. "I guess I felt like you played me."

"How?"

"I was excited to have Nina in my life at first. I didn't hold any grudges or hatred toward you until I saw the hurt in my mother's eyes. One day I overheard her talking to my aunt about how bad she felt on missing out on her first grandchild's birth, the first time she sat up, and shit just point-blank period we missed out on."

"I understand."

"Do you?"

"Yeah, I do. But I was embarrassed for what seemed like an eternity to have the only person I wanted to be with disappearing. I didn't have a number, forwarding address, or nothing. Was I supposed to go and tell everyone I was pregnant by you but didn't know where you were?"

"Maybe!"

"That's a selfish reply, Troy."

"Look, I'm sorry; I just wish you would'a told me."

"How, Troy? You left. You keep blaming me for you not being there for Nina's first year, but in reality, it was your fault. You left, you pushed me away, and you chose to leave." I tried to whisper as I noticed our voices had risen and we were starting to draw attention.

"I don't know. Maybe I'm just mad at myself." I watched him struggle with his thoughts. My stare was interrupted when the waiter came over with our plates.

"That's was quick," I said, placing my napkin in my lap and preparing for my first bite. We ate in silence. Lost in our separate thoughts.

It was a quarter after ten and still an early night, but I knew I would have to get up early to head to the lounge. Troy parked his truck in my driveway and we sat and looked at the house we used to share. It looked so empty and lifeless. I sighed in frustration. *This dinner got us nowhere.*

Troy pulled open his door and walked toward my car to open my door. "Kind of reminds me of our first time out," he said. I gave him a weak smile and walked toward my front door.

He took my keys out of my hand as I started to place them in the lock.

"What are you doing?"

"I remember when we first started dating before we had sex and all that, I wanted to always make sure there wasn't an intruder in your house. So allow me to continue on my ritual."

I rolled my eyes in annoyance and stood back so he could act like Mr. Tuff Guy. "Is there any danger among us?" I said sarcastically, throwing my purse across the couch as I entered.

"I think we are good." He started to run up the stairs two steps at a time. "I'm going to get some clothes for Nina since I have her all week, cool?"

I walked into my master room and slipped out of my shoes. Then I ran my fingers through my hair. Taking a lighter in my hand, I lit my smallest candle. *Nights like these I wish Nina was here to keep me company.* After that, I slid out of my dress, pulling it over my head, and threw myself across my bed, closing my eyes, drifting into a much-needed sleep.

TROY WASHINGTON

Walking into the house I used to share with Nitrah, I was pleased to see it was clean and just the way it was when I lived here months ago. I walked around and made sure the house was really empty and decided to get Nina some clothes for next week while I was here. The dinner with Nitrah was cool, but I still felt like we were frozen in that same spot. That spot neither of us knew exactly what it was. I loved her, but it seemed our relationship held a lot of baggage from the get-go. Maybe it was a lost cause.

I grabbed one of Nina's Disney tote bags and started to stuff it with things I knew she would want. Then I walked out of her room, glanced into the guest room, and then the office Nitrah and I used to share.

Walking down the steps I heard only silence. Nitrah had failed to turn on any lights, so I used the moonlight that was shining through the blinds to guide me through the living room. I walked to the back of the house, to the room I used to share with Nitrah, to find her lying across the bed. My mind flashed back to when Dahlia was in my bed, wearing the same amount of clothes. Or should I say, the least amount.

She was breathing deeply, so I knew she was in a deep sleep. I could remember how deep she would breathe in and out when she was in one of her deep slumbers. I used to love to watch her sleep. Maybe because she looked peaceful and the drama from the day wasn't shown all over her face. I leaned in the door frame and placed Nina's bag by the door. I just wanted to stare at her. Maybe remember how we used to be.

My mind trailed to the many times I made love to her in this room, the times Nina, Nitrah, and I would eat dinner in bed instead of at the table; how we would watch TV and wrap our arms around each other. I honestly missed that. *I got to get back here to where things do matter.*

I stood now beside the bed, my eyes trailing across Nitrah's ass. Her perfect onion-shaped cheeks were completely exposed because she wore a thong and a black one at that. My dick hardened. It wasn't easy to see because the room was almost completely dark except for the one candle she lit. I used to yell at her every night for keeping the candles lit and threatening to burn the house down. Looked like she still did what she chose. I laughed to myself at the fact that Nitrah was hardheaded.

My foot was planted in the carpet as I watched her back rise up and down. I didn't notice that I had leaned forward until I could feel her breath brush across my cheek. I leaned in and kissed her lips. Her breathing pattern stayed the same. I leaned back up and proceeded to slide out of my shoes and towered my body over Nitrah's.

I gently planted a kiss in the middle of her back. Her dark skin and smooth texture caused my dick to pulsate against the zipper of my jeans. I slid further down, trying to make the least amount of sudden moves as possible. She still lay in a deep sleep. I wanted to taste her, to see if she still held the same scent I used to love to smell. Planting my feet back on the floor, I bent down over her ass admiring its perfect form.

I trailed a finger over the crack of her ass down to her thighs, bringing my hands and placing them in the middle of her legs. She squirmed a little, but I could tell she wasn't quite awake yet.

I gently started to push her thighs apart and like the Red Sea when Moses was trying to free the Jews, her sweet nectar was starting to make its way to my presence. I hid down on the ground when Nitrah completely turned her body over, pulling the cover over her body. I leaned down so that she couldn't see me. I wanted to be like a thief in the night.

Five minutes passed, and I heard her breathing go back into its rhythmic motion. When I glanced up over the bed, Nitrah was in yet another deep sleep, but this time I smiled because she was on her back. *Perfect!*

I walked around the foot of the bed and raised up the ends of the bedsheet, putting my head under it. I could feel Nitrah's warm legs on either side, so I gently pushed them further apart to bring my face closer to the spot I wanted to taste so badly.

I could smell the perfume she must have placed there earlier today and gently kissed the top of her panties. I took my finger and pushed her panties to the side, and then kissed her lips there. I felt her move and just before she could realize I was down there, I stuck the tip of my tongue out and licked her lips, and taking my tongue, I pulled them apart and a moan escaped Nitrah's mouth.

"Troy!" she whispered. I shushed her and found her clit that was completely soft. I wrapped my lips around it and gave it a gentle pull, and it stiffened on cue. Nitrah's legs began to widen, allowing me to know she was accepting my offer to taste her. I extended my tongue to its full length and found the opening I was searching for and inserted it in with an eager thrust. Nitrah raised her ass higher to give me easier access, and I obliged the gesture by twirling my tongue around her walls and tasting her nectar as it trailed to my mouth. I went in deep, making sure my chin touch the tip of her ass, bringing my tongue out to the very last tip and doing it all over again. I made sure to keep her clit occupied with my index and thumb squeezing it roughly in between my fingers.

Nitrah started to grind her hips, and I followed her lead until I felt her legs start to shake uncontrollably. I knew she was about to have her orgasm, so I placed my fingers inside her and gave her a rough jab, pulling them in and out. She cried out for me to go harder, so I did, and when her body went limp, I gave her lips one last kiss.

***

I didn't spend the night with Nitrah. Instead, I kissed her on the forehead and made my way back to my box I called an apartment. I didn't want her to regret what we did, and I didn't want to give her the impression that we were good and back together. I just missed her, and I wanted to show her that.

In all honestly, I was confused, or maybe stuck on stupid because she was a good woman, but now I had feelings for Dahlia too. How was I supposed to hide those feelings? We hated each other, and everyone knew that, but if we all of a sudden started to act like we were friends, it would be only a matter of time before everyone knew what was up.

The season with the team was over and with it almost being June I was still in talks to coach at UTA. Meeting with Mr. Francis had placed me at the top of the list, and I was still waiting for a yes or no. I knew practice had to start in the summertime, and if I was going to be brought in, it needed to be soon.

To take away my thoughts of last night with Nitrah and with UTA, I took Robert and Tim up on their offer to go out and play some hoops. Then later, hit up a club. I needed to blow off some steam, and this was the perfect way to.

When I walked into the gym I noticed an old familiar face, Lester. He worked with Tim at the construction site and used to play ball with us, and I hadn't seen him in a few months. But he had mad game, and I made sure he was on my team. It was two on two; me and Lester against Tim and Robert. After an hour and a half of playing, we won by three points and called it quits.

"Yo', let's go over to the sausage shack. I'm hungry as hell now," Lester said in between pants.

"That's cool. I'm hungry my damn self," Robert said grabbing a towel and wiping away his sweat. After heading into the locker and putting on dry clothes, we all hopped in our cars and drove over to the sausage shack. There I felt like I was in the middle of show-and-tell as each of the guys described their latest lay. I couldn't mention last night because I really didn't want them to know. We ate our food and proceeded to make our way to our separate destinations until we met up later that night at the club.

I wore some new Capri jeans with a red shirt and a new fitted cap with the letters NY on the front. I rode with Robert since we hadn't tag teamed at the club for a while now and like brothers, his style almost reflected mine. We pulled up to Taste, a club that used to be MP3, and walked up to the bouncer who charged us twenty to get in. It was well after 11:30, and I knew that the club would be in full swing. And I was right.

With Robert trailing behind, I located Tim at the bar already talking game in a woman's ear. I gave him a head nod, and he motioned for us to come on over. Stepping up to him, I gave him a one-hand shake and ordered a Crown and Coke from the bartender, pulling out a twenty.

"Are you going to buy me a drink too?" I heard a woman's voice say. I turned around, and lo and behold, a familiar face smiled at me.

"Nitrah, what are you doing here?"

"I'm meeting the girls," she tried to yell over the music.

I leaned in to speak in her ear and said, "You know you are wrong for what you got on."

She rolled her eyes and laughed. "Ha, you the one to notice, huh?" She leaned over and gave Robert and Tim a hug.

"Is Jazz's fine ass with you?" Tim yelled out. I laughed off his comment. He always said comments to Jazz like that, as if they weren't divorced.

"Yes, Tim, she's in the bathroom. Behave tonight, all right? We didn't even know you all would be here," Nitrah said.

I took a sip of my drink and looked over Nitrah's outfit again. I started to get mad at how much of her breasts she was showing. Her dress was skintight and made her ass look bigger than what it was, and her face was beautiful. I almost got lost in her eyes when she smiled at me and said, "So you gonna buy me a drink?"

Jumping out of my trance, I turned around to the bartender to order her a drink when I noticed Robert's eyes looking at Nitrah a little too long. "Yo', bro, watch the eyes, dog," I yelled out.

"Oh, don't mind Robert. He knows a fine-ass woman when he sees one, right, Robert?" Nitrah laughed and stood next to me at the bar.

"Yo', Robert, don't answer that," I yelled out, eyeing Nitrah with my *don't play with me* look.

Jazz walked toward us and said, "Did I miss something here? I did not sign up for a blast from the past, double-date fiasco."

Tim walked over to her, giving her a bear hug. She accepted it, but it wasn't in the way Tim had hoped. "Hey, Jazz. Let me take you down memory lane on the dance floor." Tim pulled her by the hand and led her to the dance area.

"Only if you buy me a drink or two," I heard her yell out before they walked off.

"I thought you said all y'all were coming. Where's Charmaine and Dahlia?" Robert asked. I suddenly felt my stomach drop as I started to choke on my drink. Then I felt Nitrah start to pat my back.

"Damn, bro, you can't take the liquor anymore," Robert laughed before walking off as he spotted a lady he wanted to dance with.

"You all right?" Nitrah asked.

"Yeah, so where your girls at anyway?" I needed to know how long before Dahlia would be in the vicinity.

"I don't know. Dahlia's been running late for almost everything now. I think she got her a new boo, and Charmaine been struggling with her divorce and all. So they'll show up when they show up. You want to dance too?" She extended her hand, and I took it. If I had any luck, Dahlia wouldn't even show up tonight.

DAHLIA JONES

Who was I kidding? Troy was playing me like he always did, and the fact he was in Club Taste holding Nitrah's ass in his hands proved that. I should just walk my ass on home. Hell, were Troy and I seeing each other anyway? We hadn't kissed or had sex, but the time we spent together meant more to me than just a random lay. I genuinely was starting to care about him.

It was time to put the final chapters of Nitrah and Troy in motion. I had him first, and I would have him last. From the get-go, Nitrah wasn't supposed to fall for Troy, and now it was time to get back what was rightfully mine. I started to walk over when I felt a hand touch my shoulder. I turned and saw Robert.

I tried to hide my annoyance at him stopping my quest to call Troy out. "Robert!" I said dryly.

"Nice to see you too, Dahlia. I didn't know if you were coming or not." Robert was a good man. The total opposite of his brother Troy, and I used to love him at one point, but let's be honest. He could never have my heart completely because I was in love with his brother. Our last quest to make our relationship work failed after a miserable six weeks.

"Yeah, I'm late. Good to see you, though," I lied. I wanted to be let free to go and blast Troy a new one. I was pissed about him playing both fields. He needed to choose, and even if that meant losing Nitrah as a friend, I wanted to be with Troy. Deep down, I knew he wanted me too.

"I went ahead and reserved a booth for us all over there and got some wings coming too. So when you're ready, make your way over there." I nodded that I understood, and instead of heading to the dance floor to confront Troy, I went to the bar. I needed a hard drink to ease my nerves. Twenty minutes and four drinks later, I was relaxed.

"Dahlia, girl, why aren't you out here shaking that big ass of yours?" Nitrah said, walking up to me and wrapping her arms around my neck giving me a tight hug.

"Just relaxing, waiting for y'all to get off the floor. So Troy and you, huh?"

"Oh no, we're just dancing and having some fun, if you know what I mean." She laughed, and I rolled my eyes. "What, Dahlia? I know you're tired of our merry-go-round, but hey, it's us."

"Yeah, whatever. Robert got us a booth over here." I wobbled off the bench and walked back to where Robert said we were sitting. I instantly saw Troy with Robert and Tim, who was sitting a tad bit too close to Jazz. Troy looked up and saw me coming. His smile went away. *Oh, is it like that?*

He motioned for Nitrah to hurry and sit by him, and I sat on the outside. "Hey, Dahlia, you finally made it," Jazz said. I sensed some sarcasm in her voice.

"Yeah, pass me a wing, will ya?" I was sure I said that loud enough for her to hear. But she clearly ignored me. *What the hell?* Instead, Robert pushed the wing basket closer to me.

"Oh, guys, that's my cue my baby is here. I'll see y'all in a minute," Robert said, getting up from the table. I looked over and rolled my eyes at his Ashanti look-alike girlfriend.

"That's the best he can do," I smirked. The table grew silent. "What's everyone's problem tonight? Y'all in a funky mood?" I slurred.

"Yo', Dahlia, I see you're drunk. Why don't Jazz and I drive you home?" Tim asked.

"I'm fine, and hell to the no, you can't drive me home. I haven't enjoyed my time out yet," I said, eyeing Troy.

Nitrah sighed and said, "Please don't start anything tonight with Troy. I see you eyeballing him already. I thought we were past this."

"Yeah, me too, Nitrah. I thought Troy and I were finally connecting," I said sarcastically.

"OK, Ms. Thang, let's go to the bathroom and wash up." I felt Jazz push me out of my seat and wrap her hands around my waist.

I leaned into Tim and whispered, "Remember our talk the other night?" He nodded that he remembered. Then I eyed Dahlia, and then glanced toward Nitrah, telling him exactly who I was talking about without speaking it.

I felt him tense up with disbelief. "No way," he whispered back.

"That's the best he can do," I heard Dahlia say about Robert's new girlfriend.

"Yo', Dahlia, I see you're drunk. Why don't Jazz and I drive you home?" I loved Tim for moments like these. He knew just like I knew that we had to get Dahlia out of the club before shit hit the fan. But like the stubborn mule she is, she refused. I managed to push her out of the booth and walk her into the bathroom. Then I pulled out my cell phone and sent Tim a text to pull his car around. I was getting Dahlia out of here. He sent a reply and said he was way ahead of me. I smiled at our quick thinking.

It was only twenty minutes ago I allowed myself to let loose and grind my hips into his groin. But, hey, it was just dancing. There was no interest to get back to Tim at all. I had a good man. But Tim still treated me like we were casually dating. I liked how we could talk about anything and just like almost every time I saw him tonight, I was going to tell him that we were still not getting back together.

I threw some water on a paper towel and wiped Dahlia's face. Her eyes were rolling around in her head like she was possessed. "Dahlia, is you sure all you had was a few drinks? Damn." I poked my head out and motioned for a bouncer to help me carry her drunken ass out to Tim's car.

Once we got her in his car, I hopped in mine and had him follow me to her house. Once there, I took Dahlia's purse and searched for her keys and found what I was looking for and unlocked her door. Tim carried her to her bedroom and threw her across the bed.

"Damn, Tim, why so rough?" I whispered.

"If she's fucking Troy, then she deserved it. I'm going to give him a good hit too when I see him."

"Let's just get out of here." I walked back to her kitchen and opened her refrigerator and noticed she had some of my favorite drinks, Capri Suns. I grabbed the whole box. "This is my little payback for hurting my girl." I giggled and threw Tim a drink.

"Jazz, get your silly ass on out the door." He took the juice and popped his straw in it, locking the door behind us.

Once outside, I opened my juice and took a swallow. Then I reached for my cell and noticed a text from Nitrah asking where we went. I told her we took Dahlia home and I would call her tomorrow.

"Are you hungry? I know that Fina is still open and making those homemade burgers."

"Yeah, I can eat before I head back home. I'm following you." We hopped in our cars and made our way back into Fort Worth to the Southside to go to the gas station that never closed. They had a cook that made homemade burgers, wings, burritos, and chicken. After the clubs closed at three in the morning, this is where everyone went, and like clockwork with it being one in the morning, the parking lot was full.

Tim and I used to come here many times, and this brought back good memories. I parked my car and hopped in his while he went and ordered our food. Immediately, I clicked open my phone and called Charmaine.

"Hey," she said groggy.

"Hey, girl, why didn't you come out tonight?"

"Tired from working. What's up? It's late."

"I need you to meet me over at the lounge tomorrow. I need to speak to you and Nitrah together, and I can't repeat what I got to say."

"Sounds serious."

"Oh, it is. Be there at one, OK?"

"Yeah, OK. I can come on my break."

"All right, lady. I'll talk to you tomorrow. Love you." I heard a hesitation in Char's voice before she said, "I love you too."

I closed my phone wondering if there was more going on with Charmaine then she led on. *Damn, what's going on with my friends?*

RAYNE ANDERSON

"So what do you think?" I looked at my private investigator with much anticipation. The footage I had was priceless, but it needed to be edited some.

"I think we are done. The final edits look great and no one would suspect it's been edited."

I leaned in and gave him a gracious hug. And I was gracious because in less than twenty-four hours, little Ms. Jazz would have a surprise of her own. She just needed to know that she and Maxwell weren't meant to be, and I volunteered to be the messenger.

"Rayne, I'll drop this off at the bookstore first thing tomorrow morning, and then we're done. It's been a pleasure working for you." He stood and tipped his hat toward me.

"Yeah, sure. I'll call and confirm you made the delivery. I appreciate it so. Now, off we go." I gently pushed him toward my front door, shut it, then leaned against it feeling like I was on cloud nine. My baby Maxwell would come running back to me as soon as Jazz leaves him.

I still can't understand why he chose her over me. I mean, look at me with my perfectly round 38 DD breasts, video-vixen ass, tight abs, and more hips for days. I was the prime model for the glass Coke bottle. I walked up to my room dropping my own version of the video into my DVD player.

Instantly that day started to replay with my mouth around Maxwell's shaft. His thick long dick pulsated inside my mouth. I loved seeing the reaction of pleasure all over his face. He loved me. I just had to make him admit it.

CHARMAINE WRIGHT

It was my lunch time, and surprisingly for a Monday it wasn't as busy as I had thought it would be. I logged out of my desk computer, popped my head into my director's office, and told him I would be back in two hours. I got on the highway after first grabbing a burger and headed toward Nitrah's lounge, wondering what news Jazz had to share.

As I pulled up, I noticed that Dahlia was the only one missing. *Dang, she is always late; I got to get back to work on time.*

Inside, a few patrons were eating and dining. Jazz was sitting at the bar area. She called out Nitrah's name before I had a chance to make it any further. "Hey, Jazz." I leaned in and gave her a hug and proceeded to do the same thing when Nitrah came out.

"All right, ladies, follow me up to the balcony, will ya?" Jazz said. Once upstairs, I sat in one of the cushy cushions and crossed my legs patiently waiting for Jazz to say what she had to say so I could go on about my business.

"Where is Dahlia, and why isn't she a part of this discussion?" Nitrah asked.

"Look, I know we got a busy day ahead, but I couldn't go another week knowing what I know." Jazz stared at Nitrah.

Nitrah instantly took on her nervous stare and said, "What's wrong? What happened now?"

"Last week I went to go surprise Dahlia for lunch, and *I* ended up getting a surprise myself."

"What?" I quizzed, now obviously curious that it involved a secret around our best friend.

"She's dating someone now," Jazz said. I blew out aggravated air.

"Jazz, I *do* have a job, you know. I can't just be taking off to talk about Dahlia's love life."

"I'm with Charmaine on this," Nitrah said, leaning back in her chair, crossing her arms. She was clearly annoyed as was I.

"Ladies, the problem is *who* she's dating and how it will change everything."

Jazz looked toward Nitrah again. I covered my mouth in shock, clearly getting the fact that Jazz was insinuating that Dahlia was dating someone Nitrah used to be with.

"Oh my goodness. Dahlia is creeping with an ex of mine?" Nitrah yelled out. She looked around her lounge to make sure no one heard her.

"I'm afraid so," Jazz said.

"Who?" I asked eagerly to know and clearly in shock.

"Nitrah, you got to understand that after I tell you this, you must think first and react later."

"Damn, Jazz, who is it? It must be a man I really care about. Dahlia wouldn't do this to me. Maybe it's a mistake."

"No, it's not mistake because these two are known for hating each other, and what I saw was genuine like for each other. They were touching and hugging and flirting."

Nitrah pulled at her hair in frustration. "Who the fuck was it, Jazz?"

A long pause followed, with suffocating silence. I think the entire room went into slow motion and we all were in a trance. I watched Jazz open her mouth, and I was on the edge of my seat; my stomach was in knots, and my head was ringing.

"Troy!" I think the air left my lungs.

"No," I said a bit above a whisper.

"What!" Nitrah exclaimed. Her reaction was a shocking one. She sat calmly, but her face was full of confusion.

"I saw Dahlia and Troy together. This is why I had to get her out of the club last night because she was upset that Troy and you were all up on each other."

"No, Jazz, you got to be mistaken. Troy despises Dahlia. They can't stand each other. They wouldn't."

"But they do, and they did," Jazz said.

"I don't believe this. Why would those two of all people do a 180?" I asked.

"No, this can't be. Troy and I were just together the other night. He wouldn't even dare try to play me like that. He wouldn't hurt me like that. We have Nina," Nitrah cried.

Jazz and I walked over to her and bent down on our knees, each taking a shoulder of hers to rub. I couldn't believe this was happening, and to top this shit off, I was a backstabbing friend too. This was also my fate.

"I'm sorry, Nitrah. I only held this a secret from you for a couple of days. I talked to Tim about it, but I didn't tell him who I was talking about, and he said to keep quiet. But I knew I would be wrong if I did. I know you would tell me if it were me."

I swallowed real hard at Jazz's statement. Would I be exposed next just like Dahlia was now?

"I can not believe this is happening. First, Denim; then, Troy; then, Michael; then Troy again. When will I finally find someone to love me?" Nitrah screamed. "I'm going to pay that bitch Dahlia a visit."

I sighed and dropped to the floor, sitting Indian-style. "I'm tired of all this. If you think back, this shit started three years ago this month when Dahlia came up with this bright idea for you, Nitrah, to date Troy and break his heart. Y'all dumb asses went along with it when I said no. To top this shit off, you and Troy go back and forth with a rocky relationship for two years, and then in the end, you two have a child together.

Now, Dahlia comes back and does this. And me, I got all this …" I trailed off.

"What?" Jazz asked.

I stood up on my feet and grabbed my purse. "I got to go. I'm just taken aback by this news. I love you all, but we all got baggage, and I just need some time alone. You understand, right? I got to focus on my divorce finalizing, and I need support not drama."

"Oh, so you bailing out on us, Char?" Nitrah yelled.

"Nitrah and Jazz, I love you both. Give me some time, okay?" I hugged them both and walked out of the lounge completely in cry-baby mode. Tears stung my eyes as I tried to wipe them away and open my car door. Once inside, I screamed at the top of my lungs. Everything was not what it was supposed to be. How was I going to tell Jazz that I had been sleeping with Tim long before she had?

After helping Nitrah leave and go home for the day, I made her promise not to say anything to Troy or Dahlia until I spoke to Tim again. I knew she was hurt, but in the end, knowing was better. I mean, we were talking about two best friends involved with the same man; of course I had to say something.

Making my way back to the store, I waved at my manager and made my way back to the office. Poking her head in my office door my manager said, "You got a package while you were out."

I noticed the yellow envelope on my desk and nodded my head okay. I cut my computer on and logged into my accounting program to get back to work. While it rebooted, I took the envelope in my hand and noticed it wasn't stamped.

"Hey, did someone drop this off?" I yelled out.

"Yes, some white guy."

Curiously, I opened its contents and only a blank DVD fell out. *What is this*? I opened the disk and placed it in my hard drive. I heard it start to run and my Windows Media window popped up.

I pressed play, and then my phone rang. I hurriedly pressed paused and picked up the phone. "Jazzy Reads."

"Hey, Jazz, baby, what are you doing?"

"Hey, Maxy. I love when you call me that." I smiled from ear to ear, excited to hear the voice of the man I loved so much ringing in my ear.

"So what are you doing in say about an hour?"

"Hopefully, lunch and dessert with you," I laughed. I leaned back in my chair and took my mouse in my hand as Maxwell started to narrate his day at the construction site of his new restaurant. I knew how this was going to go. He was so excited about this that mostly he would ramble off at the mouth and be talking for a good ten minutes without my having to reply. I always halfway listened and occasionally said "uh-huh" just so he would think I was listening. I loved him, but listening about a building being built and all his floor plans was boring.

I took my mouse and pressed play on the mysterious video and sat back in my chair listening to Maxwell ramble off. The screen was black. *Great, a blank disk. Who would send me this crap?*

I leaned forward to press exit when Maxwell's voice started to play. But the screen was still blank. *What the hell is this? Is Maxwell surprising me with another gift?*

That thought quickly left my mind when I heard a woman's voice. Then the screen went clear. I could see as clear as day Maxwell sitting on a couch receiving oral sex from Rayne. I screamed out.

"Baby, what's wrong? Wait, is Rayne over there again?" I blocked his voice out as I sat stunned and watched my world crumble. Rayne stood up, her dress showing she had on no panties, and straddled Maxwell. When she started to have sex with him by grinding her hips into his groin I hurriedly pressed the power button off on my computer.

"Jazz, baby, do you hear me? Is everything all right?" I heard Maxwell's voice from afar, then I remembered I was on the phone with him.

I picked it up and placed it back to my ear. Tears slowly dropped from my eyes as I said, "You fucked her."

"What? Wait, baby, what's going on?"

"Maxwell, come on, tell me the truth." I was crying so hard I barely recognized my own voice.

"No, baby, wait. Is she telling you this?"

"Tell me, Max, from your own mouth."

"I'm on my way over there, Jazz."

"Don't bother. I won't be here." I slammed the phone down and threw my head on my desk and cried into my arms. I wasn't thinking, and the only thing I felt was pain and agony. *He was supposed to be different.*

I ran out of my office, wiping my face, and told my manager to close up tonight. Then I hopped in my SUV and sped off. I didn't know where to go. Nitrah was at home crying her eyes out, and I didn't want to burden her with my drama.

Char had just disowned us, and now Max. *I loved him more than I ever loved Tim.*

I knew one place I could go. That was Mama's house.

Less then thirty minutes later I pulled up in front of my mother's house and used my key to go in.

"Who's that at the door?" Mama called out.

"It's me, Mama."

"Jazz, aren't you supposed to be at the store?" She walked out from the kitchen in her bathrobe.

"Middle of the day, Mama, and you still ain't got any clothes on," I said dryly, plopping myself on her couch.

She walked over toward me sitting in her favorite seat that was beside the couch. I knew she was reading me. That's what she always did. She mostly sensed when things were wrong before you actually told her.

"So, whatever done happened? You over here now. You going to tell me what's wrong or are you going to pout and poke your lip out until it's numb?"

"Mama, I really thought Maxwell was the one."

"What done happened now in the time y'all been together anyhow? It hasn't even been a year yet. Did you give your relationship some time before you started declaring marriage in the future to him?"

"Well …"

"Exactly. Y'all was this instant couple from day one. Right before your divorce was finalized. Had little ole Tim hoping and crying you'll take him back, but you were stuck on Mr. New Guy."

"So you think I made a mistake?" I sighed.

"I'm not saying what I think you should have done. Maxwell is a good man. I know he loves you, and he's older, more stable; and best of all, he loves that boy of yours."

"That's not enough for him to sleep with his ex, Mama. Someone sent me a video of them having sex."

"Oh, really now?" Mama said getting up and walking back into the kitchen. I got up and followed her, wanting to know what her reply to that was.

"Nothing to say now, Mama?"

"What would you want me to say?"

"No, I want you to say what's on your mind." I took a seat at her table and watched her go back to the frying pan where she was frying chicken.

"Jazz, you so headstrong that when a man fails you up, you leave and hop on the next train, only to discover most men are the same. Now if this Maxwell really is trying to hurt you on purpose, then I would advise you to leave. But always think about your actions before you perform them, sugar."

"So, what you mean? All men cheat?"

"Not men, Jazz; people fail sometimes. No one is perfect."

"Cheating is the ultimate no-no, Mama."

"Oh, really?"

"Yes, really. It's not only cheating physically, but it's cheating someone out of happiness and breaking their heart. There's no coming back from that."

"This video you say was sent to you, right?"

"Yes."

"Do you know from whom?"

"No."

"I know Maxwell wouldn't send such a thing. So think about who would send it and why." *Damn, Mama had a point.*

"I've met the woman. She told me her intentions to be with Maxwell." All Mama did was nod her head in the process of dropping another piece of chicken in the fryer.

"Now all you need to do is talk to the man. See why he did what he did and if he wants to be in a relationship with you. Pretty simple, baby. One thing any woman wants is a good man, and many will do anything to get that good man. And even though this is a horrible situation, I feel in my heart that this one here is a good man. I mean, Tim wasn't bad either, but hey, who am I say." She laughed. I threw a dish towel her way and laughed along with her.

"I'm still hurt, Mama."

"I know sugar. But talk to the man, and if he is as good as I say he is, then he will be at your beck and call until you have forgiven him. Sounds like to me he was set up anyway."

"There isn't such thing as his d … I mean his penis accidentally going inside of someone."

"All right, gal, watch your mouth around me. I'll jump over this here counter and wash that mouth out."

I laughed and said, "Sorry, Mama. I'm going to let him squirm for a while, then I'll talk to him. I've waited a long time for a fulfilling relationship, and I finally feel that love knows me and I know it."

"Do that, and while you're at it, start peeling these here potatoes. I want some homemade fries too."

I picked up the phone and dialed Tim's number, letting him know that after the day I had I was picking up Junior and taking him out to have some pizza. Ironically, Tim was off early and offered to go along with us. "I don't have anything to do either," he said. I rolled my eyes in annoyance and said okay.

After purposely turning my phone off, I strapped Junior in his car seat and hopped in the passenger seat of Tim's truck. Tim was grinning a little too hard.

"Why do you do that?" I asked

"Do what?"

"Make this out to be more than what it is?"

"I'm just happy to see my family. Is that a problem?" He licked his lips the way I used to like it when we were together and I rolled my eyes in annoyance again. "Jazz, why do you always roll your eyes at me as if I don't see that?"

"Oh, I want you to see. Can we just have a platonic night out with our son and enjoy some pizza?"

"OK, Jazz. I get it that you don't want to be with me. Damn, do you have to remind me every time I see you?" I glanced toward him and saw I had truly hurt his feelings. I couldn't ever let him know that Maxwell cheated on me. I hadn't spoken to him since I saw the video only a few hours ago, and I already knew I didn't have any intentions on letting Rayne get what she wanted. And that meant forgiving Maxwell. If Tim ever found out, he would go crazy and all hell would break loose. *How can you forgive him and not me?* I could hear it now.

"I spoke to Nitrah earlier today," I said.

"You told her, didn't you?" I nodded my head yes. "Damn, now I got to go and give Troy a heads-up. That is, if Nitrah ain't gone and took a damn brick to his truck already. You can't hold water, Jazz."

"I'm a friend, and if it were me, then I would want to know. You would do the same for me, wouldn't you?"

Tim grew silent.

"Yeah, I would," he finally stuttered.

"Don't play with me, Tim. I know you'd have my back if it came down to it."

"Come on, Jazz, you know I wouldn't hurt you like that," he said looking into my eyes. I saw the sincerity that he had, and I knew in my heart he wouldn't betray me like Dahlia did Nitrah.

TROY WASHINGTON

I stood there almost a whole ten minutes now waiting on Dahlia to open the door. I called out Dahlia's name again. I knew she was home; her car was sitting directly in the driveway. "I'm not leaving until you open this door." I knew that last night Dahlia was upset. But what was I supposed to do? I was supposed to be with Nitrah and not with her.

She pulled opened the door and yelled, "Do I need to call the cops?" I pushed past her and walked into her house.

"Don't go acting like the old Dahlia again. You know damn well you aren't going to call the cops."

"What do you want?" she said, slamming the door closed.

"I know you're upset about last night. But what else did you expect me to do? Nitrah and I aren't actually on bad terms now, and me and you—well, let's just say we are this well-kept secret."

She plopped down on the sofa beside me. "What do you expect me to do while you go off and do whatever?"

I felt genuine care in her voice. I was confused on what to really tell her. "Dahlia, I honestly don't know. We got to tread careful on this, you know."

"Are we together, or aren't we together?" *There goes the ultimate question.*

"I want to be. Honestly, I do. But my daughter and her well-being come first. I can't have a toxic relationship with her mother. And to be honest, I still care about Nitrah."

"Sure you do," Dahlia whispered.

"What do you want me to say?"

"It's not what I want you to say, it's what you need to say."

"And that is exactly …?"

"I want to be with you in more ways than one." She took my hand and placed it on her chest. I felt the beating of her heart. "Do you feel that? That's my heart beating for you."

Damn! I was at a loss for words. I sat there and looked at her with a blank stare; one, not wanting to say the wrong thing, and two, not wanting to make the wrong move. She leaned toward me and that's when I knew she was going in for the kiss. *Should I move or should I just let it be?*

I leaned back on the sofa as Dahlia rose up and straddled me. She leaned down, and I could feel the warm heat from her mouth inches away from mine. I suddenly became anxious to kiss the woman I hadn't touched this way since college. I raised my head toward hers, taking my hands and placing them on both sides of her face, bringing her lips down to mine. *Soft,* I thought as I began to tease and nibble at her bottom lip. I could feel her body tense up.

"Troy, would you follow me to my bedroom?" I looked up into her face and read her expression. *Did I want to take it there with her? There would be no turning back.*

She rose up and reached for my hand. I gave it to her. I stood up from the couch and followed her down the hallway into her bedroom. I started to feel the pulsation that made me rise with anticipation. I stood in her doorway and watched her remove her shirt.

There she was in a white bra and small cotton shorts and motioned for me to walk over to her. I did. I pulled my shirt over my head and leaned down to kiss her again. The heat I felt between us was unbearable as I took my hands and trailed it down to her ass, giving it a tight squeeze. I pushed her down on the bed and towered myself over her body, trailing my hands over her small stomach down to her shorts, sliding my hand under them. Opening her legs, my hand found its way to her clit giving it a tight squeeze. She arched her back, pushing her hips toward me. I reached down with both hands, pulling her shorts to the floor, and spreading her legs eagle-style.

Removing the remainder of our garments, we got lost in each other's kiss. Our motions started to increase. After protecting myself, I raised her leg over my shoulder and slowly made my way into her opening, sliding myself in deep. The first time I was inside her was so intense we collapsed on each other in a matter of minutes. I instantly grabbed another condom, strapped up, and went in for round two.

MAXWELL WAYNE

It was close to midnight and neither Jazz nor Junior was home. I had called the day care and discovered he was picked up early. I knew Jazz could only be in certain places like the store, at Nitrah's lounge, out with her friends, or at her mother's. I hadn't had the chance to really get to know her mother and decided just to drive by instead of knocking. She wasn't there either, just like every other place I looked. I couldn't believe Rayne set me up.

After Jazz hung up on me, I went to the store. Her manager said she ran out of there after receiving a package that had been dropped off earlier. Going into her back office, I saw the contents on her desk and found the disk still in her computer. There I saw the video that would end everything I ever had with Jazz. Rayne set me up!

My next intention was to confront Rayne, but she had mysteriously ignored my phone calls all day. She knew I wanted to confront her. *Damn, I hate that woman*. The nerve of her breaking up my relationship when she was the one who left me and moved to Washington, D.C. I didn't know what else to do but go home and wait for Jazz.

When one thirty in the morning rolled around, I saw headlights pull into our driveway and then the garage door opened. It was Jazz pulling in. I sat up on the couch and braced myself for whatever came. I heard her unlock the door that led to the kitchen and drop her keys on the counter. I glanced back from the couch and noticed she was carrying Junior. In a dark room I imagined she couldn't see me. She walked straight toward the stairs and headed for Junior's room.

Fifteen minutes rolled by and I decided to get up and walk up the stairs to see where she was. I found her lying across the bed with Junior. I stood in the doorway and watched them. They were my life, and I couldn't lose them. I began to get emotional, wondering what was going on in Jazz's head and if she planned to leave me. I was prepared to do anything I needed to do to make her believe I wouldn't do anything like this again. But then I remembered she left her ex-husband without blinking twice when he cheated. Why wouldn't she do the same to me?

I walked in and sat down on the floor and leaned up against the wall watching the family I wanted to make mine for a lifetime. I wanted Jazz to be my wife; I wanted Junior to be my son; and I wanted to have more children.

I noticed Jazz move an inch, and so I whispered her name. She looked up and stared directly my way. "It's late," was all she said. Her voice held no compassion. It was damn near cold, and my heart crumbled at the fact that she was already looking at me differently. *But I'm still the same man you fell in love with.*

"I love you," I whispered back. "Please, Jazz, don't leave me over my mistake." She said nothing. I stared in her direction, but with the room almost completely dark I couldn't tell if her eyes were open or not. "I'm going to stay right here. I don't want anyone else."

I waited for her reply but after ten more minutes of silence I began to believe she had fallen asleep. I leaned down and placed my head on the carpet, and in a matter of minutes, I had fallen asleep too.

I woke up to see Junior's bed empty. I started to panic, thinking Jazz had taken him and left. I raced down the stairs to hear voices coming from the kitchen. It was them. I walked in timidly and said, "Good morning." Junior jumped into my arms, wrapping his small arms around my neck. Moments like these are what I lived for. I eyed Jazz, who hadn't taken her eyes off the eggs she was cooking.

"Hey, little man. Are you almost ready for school today?" Junior nodded his head yes.

I walked over and stood next to the stove, not taking my eyes off of Jazz. "Morning, Jazz, baby." She gave me nothing. I walked over and placed Junior back in his chair and grabbed some cups to pour juice in. I decided to tread lightly with Jazz, not wanting her to lash out in front of the baby.

We got through breakfast without a word to each other. Then she grabbed her purse and Junior's backpack and went to the garage door. I called out, "I love you." Her stride didn't change. Junior, however, gave me a hug good-bye, and once again, I was in the house alone. I hated this feeling.

I went toward the counter and picked up my cell and dialed Rayne's number again. This time she picked up on the third ring.

"Hey, baby."

"Rayne, I'm going to tell you this one time only. If I see you again, I will throw your head into the wall, and don't take my threat lightly. Come around me and my family, and I will fuck you up." I slammed my phone shut and stared at it. Those brief seconds had raised my blood pressure to an all-time high, and my breathing was rapid. I wanted nothing more than harm to come to Rayne right now, and I wasn't the type of person to wish that on anyone. But today was an exception.

NITRAH HILL

My phone had rung, scaring me out of my deep thoughts. Nina was at the foot of the bed watching her favorite cartoon while I, on the other hand, stared up at the ceiling.

I reached over and saw my caller ID read Jazz's number. I knew she was being sweet by checking in on me, but I didn't want to be bothered. I didn't want to talk yesterday when she told me, and I didn't want to talk now. I glanced toward Nina to make sure she was all right and rose up from the bed walking into the kitchen.

After pouring juice into my cup, I walked toward the backyard patio to let some of the wind blow on my skin. I needed to just release some tension. *A trip away from Fort Worth is what I need.*

I took another sip as I heard my house phone ring again for the tenth time this morning. I was agitated as I walked over to it and looked at the caller ID. *Speak of the devil.*

I pressed my speaker button. "What?"

"Well, good morning to you too. Why is Nina over there and not over here with me? It's my turn, remember?"

"Change in plans," I said dryly.

"What do you mean change in plans. You have her all week long. I'm not trying to go back and forth with you over this. I mean, what's up? We were just fine a couple days ago."

"Look, I have to go. And honestly, if I continue to talk to you right now, I'm going to go off. Go fuck yourself, Troy."

Click.

I started to think of who I could call about this situation. How would I confront Troy about his double dipping, and lastly, how do I let go of a person who was supposed to be my best friend? The more I thought about it, the angrier I got, the more betrayed I felt.

I set my cup of juice down and walked into the garage to get Nina's stroller. A jog in the park is what I needed, and lately, I've been slacking on that too.

After dressing Nina and getting into my workout gear, we headed straight to the nearest lake to walk its trail. I brought some old bread with me just for Nina to feed the ducks while we were out there.

It was a good thing I decided to come out early because it was still cool. The park was fairly empty, so Nina and I had the ducks to ourselves. From behind me I heard someone say, "Wow, my son was afraid of the ducks." I stood up and turned toward the voice.

"Oh, I'm sorry. Thinking out loud, I guess," the voice continued.

"That's fine. My daughter loves the ducks. How old is your son?" I said, looking down at his stroller where his son was sound asleep.

"He's two and a half. I can tell your daughter is younger and is already showing my son up. We got to change that, son," he said, looking down at the boy. I laughed a little and watched him talk to his sleeping son.

He extended his hand and said, "Sorry about that. I'm Cedric. Most people call me Ced."

"Nice to meet you, Ced. This is my daughter Nina, and I'm Nitrah. How long have you been coming to this park?" I was curious because I hadn't noticed him before, and I would have noticed such a fine specimen. He stood about six feet, fairly built, chocolate skin like mine, and his hair was cut in a low fade. Very up to my standards.

"Only a couple times before. We just moved here a couple weeks ago from Houston."

"Just you two?" I asked, wondering if he was married.

"Yep, just me and little man. Hey, why don't I give you my number? Maybe one day we can all go out. Just the four of us."

I took his business card and nodded. "Yeah, we can make that happen." I smiled toward him and held small talk before he took off in the opposite direction. Then I turned back and leaned down toward Nina admiring her laughing at the ducks. *Maybe this Ced can keep my mind off your daddy.*

TROY WASHINGTON

Something was up, but I didn't want to play guessing games with Nitrah. I hadn't called her house in two days since she hung up on me, but right about now, I was missing Nina. I subconsciously took a leave of absence from my two ladies' lives because of my hidden guilt. I had slept with Dahlia.

Don't get me wrong. The sex was good, but just like any other sticky situation, once the sex was done, reality set in. I hadn't even asked Dahlia how she'd been acting around Nitrah because I was afraid to bring up her name. Now here I was on my way to show up at Nitrah's house unexpected.

I pulled up and parked alongside the house, not wanting her to know I was there just yet by pulling into the driveway. I took a deep breath and opened my door and walked the aisle leading up to her front door. Then I pushed the doorbell and awaited the fate of this surprise meeting.

Five minutes passed by and after two more pushes of the doorbell, no reply. I decided to take my key out and let myself in. The house had an eerie quiet feeling as I stuck my head in. I whispered hello and still no reply. I walked in, closing the door behind me, and locked it.

I started to hear sounds of music. *Nitrah must be in the back listening to her stereo.* I walked toward the bedroom I used to share with her, and the music grew louder. I knew then that she was in here. I poked my head into the bedroom, and it was completely dark. I saw a light peek from under the bathroom door and the sound of Anita Baker was crooning in the air.

I went toward the door and knocked gently. No reply. I turned the knob and pushed it open lightly and the steam from the water instantly hit me. I looked around the door toward the garden tub and saw Nitrah. I stepped in and admired her completely in awe. She lay in the tub still, the bubbles and jets covered her completely.

I stood quietly, not wanting to startle her. Then she whimpered. I frowned at witnessing her like this. "Nitrah," I whispered.

She jumped and looked toward me. "What are you doing in here?" She brought her hands to her body and started to cover herself. *Why would she hide herself from me? She has never done that before.*

"I came to see you."

"How did you get in?"

"What's wrong with you?"

She rolled her eyes and sank back into the bathwater. "Why would you all of a sudden care?"

"I came to see you and Nina and to see what was wrong."

"You *really* have to ask that question?"

"I'm here, aren't I?" I said, sitting down on the toilet seat.

"Troy, just leave."

"Nitrah, talk to me. What's wrong with you and with us?"

"How can you seriously look me in the eyes and ask me that, Troy? I thought we were going to be together forever. To finally be happy, you, Nina, and me."

"I still want that."

"Yeah, *right*," she said sarcastically.

"Nitrah—"

"What the fuck do you want, Troy? I'm waiting for you to tell me. To be up front with me. To finally tell me that you don't want to be with me."

"But I do."

"And?"

"And what?"

She threw her hands up in the hand. "If you do not sit there and be honest with me, I'm going to seriously hurt the shit out of you."

"What do you want me to say?"

She stared blankly at me. I tried to read her reaction but wasn't sure what she was looking for me to say.

She looked behind her and eyed a candleholder. She reached for it and leaned up, throwing it directly at my head. I ducked in time for it to miss me. It hit the wall directly behind me.

"Get out!" she screamed.

"Are you crazy?" I yelled furiously. I was in complete shock. Nitrah's expression was pure rage. *What's going on?*

She eyed another candleholder and reached for it. I ducked and ran out the bathroom. "Nitrah, I'll come back when you calm down."

"Don't bother. Just leave me alone for good. Get the fuck out."

"What do you mean for good? Nitrah, baby ..."

"Don't baby me." I could hear her stepping out of the tub, and I proceeded to walk backward out of her bedroom.

She appeared in the bathroom doorway with a towel wrapped around her and the candleholder in her hand. She threw it where I stood, and I jumped back.

Holding up my hands in surrender, I ducked and dodged her aim and ran toward the front door. I heard Nitrah on my heels, and I didn't want to risk her catching me. I pulled open the front door and slammed it behind me.

Breathing heavily, I tried to recap what had just happened. I hopped in my truck confused about why she wanted to fight me. Why all of a sudden were Nitrah and I so far apart, or was it that she knew about Dahlia and me?

My desires were going to come true regardless, and I knew it. Sleeping with Troy only justified my feelings for him. I was in love again. Now came the question of when I was going to tell my girls. I hadn't noticed until just now that I hadn't spoken to any of them in almost a week. That's wasn't like us. After work today, I had decided I'd go meet up with Jazz at her store and walk over to Nitrah's lounge.

Of course, I'm supposed to not be around the woman who I'm trying to cut out of my man's life, but until I put my plan in motion I had to act normal. After all, I had him first, and I'll have him last. Picking up my purse to walk out of my office door, I felt my cell phone vibrate, so I pulled it out.

"Hello."

"Hey, sis, what are you up to?" Joyclyn's voice rang through my receiver. The only time she usually called in a good mood was because she needed something.

"Is there something you need, Joy? I'm heading out of the office."

"I just wanted to check on my big sis, you know. I haven't heard from you all last week. Who has you busy?"

"No one, and why, all of a sudden, do you sound cheery?"

"Well, I thought you should know your girl Charmaine is about to hit the fan."

"What do you mean, 'hit the fan'?"

"Her little secret is about to come to light."

Stopping just before I reached the elevator, I said, "What secret and how would you know?"

"Let's just say a little birdie told me." She laughed. I rolled my eyes and hung up on her. Then I dialed Charmaine's number and was surprised to get the operator who said it was disconnected. *What the hell is really going on?*

Making it into the parking garage, I got into my car and headed straight for Jazz's store. I wondered if I was out of the loop on some much-needed scoop. I made it to Jazz's place sooner than expected as I hopped out of the car and walked toward her main entrance.

Opening the door I yelled out, "Jazz, baby girl, where are you?"

A moment later she walked out and I expected to see a bright smile on her face since we hadn't talked in a week. But it was just the opposite because she clearly had an attitude.

"Hey, Jazz, what's up with you? Why haven't I heard from you?"

"I'm a little busy, so what can I do for you?"

"OK, something is clearly up. Joyclyn calls me with some weird news saying Charmaine has a secret and her phone is now disconnected, and now I see that you clearly aren't happy to see me."

"I don't know what's going on with Char, but right now, I'll just have to hold my tongue until I have been told to speak." I turned around when I heard the door open and saw Tim and Tim Junior walk in.

"Oh, hey, Dahlia, what's up?" Tim said.

"Clearly something I don't know. Jazz, what's up?" I turned back toward her and crossed my arms around my chest, tapping my foot.

"Tim, get her out of my face before I say something."

Wait! She has a problem with me. Now it's starting to make more sense. "Oh, I see, Jazz, you have a problem with me. Well, why don't you let me in on the problem so I can know too?"

Tim walked between us and said, "No, Dahlia, I think it's best that you go ahead and leave."

"Am I missing something here?" I turned around once I heard the door open again and Nitrah walked in.

"Just the bitch I wanted to see. How the fuck you show up like you have nothing to hide, as if your shit don't stink?"

Throwing my hands in the air in surrender, I said, "Wait a minute. Why is everyone ganging up on me?"

Nitrah said, "I promised myself I wasn't going to touch you, but the fact that you stand here in my face and act innocent is about to change everything. You fucking Troy!"

My face must have given away the fact that I was guilty as charged. But I wondered how the hell my girls knew. Backing up into a bookshelf I said, "Now wait a minute. Hear me out, y'all."

"Dahlia, get the hell out of my store," Jazz yelled. Nitrah walked over toward me and stood inches away from my nose.

"Really, Dahlia? You fuck Troy, the father of my child? The one I want to spend the rest of my life with?"

Stuttering, I protested, "Nitrah, it wasn't planned. Trust me. But I had him first. You knew that two years ago when you started this." I didn't see the hand rise, but I felt the stinging of her slap seconds after her hand left my face.

Tim ran up between us to push Nitrah away. I brought my hand to my face and covered the red welt that was starting to appear. "Are you crazy for hitting me?"

Nitrah was full or rage. Her chest was heaving as she breathed heavily. I tried to take control of the situation by watching what I said.

"You deserve every hit Nitrah gives you," Jazz said running up behind Tim and swinging her arm toward me, landing a blow to my back. I looked up and noticed Nitrah was coming in for another blow. Then I felt Tim pick me up by my waist as I tried to restrain Nitrah's hands as she threw fist after fist at me.

"Hey, back up, Nitrah. Jazz, open the front door," Tim tried to yell over Nitrah's screaming. I covered my face until I felt the outside heat hit my skin. Tim dropped me on to my feet. "Dahlia, get out, and I don't expect you to be coming back anytime soon."

I couldn't look him in the eyes as I had just realized that my two best friends fought me. They had a good reason to. I didn't fight Nitrah when she decided to date Troy seriously, but I knew these circumstances were different.

Upset, I opened my car door and got in, then opened the visor to look at my disheveled hair. My makeup was running down my face, and I noticed a few cuts and bruises. *Damn!*

I drove out of Jazz's store driveway without taking another look in their direction and pulled out my cell phone. I dialed the only person I knew would get my situation.

"Hello," Troy said answering.

"Troy, you better get ready because the shit has hit the fan. They know about us."

Never had I ever declared that I didn't want to be with Nitrah again in my lifetime. I was struggling with forgiving her, but I never took away the option of us being together for good. But then Dahlia happened. Her voice telling me that Nitrah knew explained everything that I needed to know about her kicking me out of the house the other night. Our journey was coming to a halt.

Panicking after I had hung up with Dahlia, I waited for Nitrah to call my phone, but after two hours had passed, I figured she wouldn't. I put on some pants and a shirt and grabbed my keys to head to Robert's house. I had to talk to him and let him know what I had gotten myself into.

He opened the door, clearly confused about why I just popped over at his house. "Bro, I need to talk to you." I looked back over his shoulder and noticed he had his lady over. "Is it a bad time?"

"No, bro, come on in. It must be important if you didn't call me first. Walk with me to the back."

Making it into his entertainment room I took a seat on the couch and took a deep breath. "Damn, bro, what's up? You're over there sweating bullets."

"I fucked up and bad."

"What do you mean?"

I didn't look his way but turned toward his 50-inch plasma television and took another deep breath. "I fucked up bad this time, and I don't know if I can get out of it."

"What did you do?"

I gave him the *I am guilty* look and turned away again. I was embarrassed to say that I had slipped back up with Dahlia—and with the woman he once was in love with.

"I see it got something to do with me. What did you do, bro?"

"I started seeing Dahlia." Robert looked at me as if he thought I were playing.

"Seriously?" he questioned.

"Yes, seriously. I fucked up and had sex with Dahlia."

"Wait a minute, when did this all happen?" He stood to his feet, his expression showing he was confused and agitated. I replayed the story to him on how I saw her at Wing Stop, how we went to the party together, and how she had changed.

"Bro, you are lucky I don't have feelings for that woman anymore. But honestly, dog, I don't feel sorry for you. You made your bed, now lie in it. Did you think of Nina when you were fucking? Hell, no. Now you come to me with this shit because you know Nitrah is done with you after this. Ain't no going back, bro."

"Robert, man, I know this. I've been struggling with this since Dahlia told me she, Jazz, and Nitrah got into a fight."

"So she knows and Jazz knows. So now everyone is about to know. Troy, do you see what you have done? You have a child with Nitrah, and now what? What are you going to do now?"

Placing my head into my heads, I rubbed my throbbing temples. "I don't know, man. That's why I came here."

"You know I love you, bro, but I ain't got your back on this one. You are on your own." He walked over toward his minifridge and pulled out two beers and handed me one.

I knocked on the door, noticing that I was knocking softer than normal, afraid of what was behind the door. I needed to speak to Nitrah sooner than later, and after finding out Nina was over at my mother's, now felt like the best time.

I heard the locks click, and I instantly became nervous about her reaction to my standing here. When the door didn't open, I placed my hand on the knob and turned it. It was unlocked.

I called her name and poked my head in. She wasn't standing at the door. *What if this is a trap?* I stepped in and quietly closed the door behind me.

"I have the remainder of your things over here," I heard her say.

I looked over toward the living room and saw a few boxes piled up. "These are my things?" I asked clueless.

"Yep." She plopped down on the couch and curled her feet under her thighs, picked up a cup, and took a sip.

"You packed all my things?"

"Yes." She didn't look in my direction as she gave me short answers. Her expression was blank, and I couldn't read her.

"Nitrah—" I started to say before I was cut off.

"Nitrah, *what*, Troy? Just get your things and leave. I'm tired of this. I'm tired of us. I don't want you anymore." That statement tugged at my heart, and I suddenly felt weak at the knees. *Damn, I fucked up this time.*

"I don't know what to say, Nitrah. I messed up, and I know there isn't any coming back from the mistakes I made." I walked over toward the first box and proceeded to pick it up. *I don't want this to be the last thing she hears from me.* I dropped the box at my feet and rushed over toward her on the couch.

"Troy, don't come near me." Her face scrunched up as if I stank or had a disease.

"Nitrah, I fucked up. I'm sorry and I don't know what to do or say. I love you, though."

She gave me a sarcastic laugh and said, "Troy, your words don't affect me anymore. Can't you see I'm finally free from you? Now if you don't get the hell out of my face, this right here is going to come charging at you." She lifted a knife that was lying by her thigh, and I jumped out of fear.

Holding up my hands in surrender I said, "OK, Nitrah, calm down. I'll get my things and leave, but we got to talk. Please, Nitrah." I walked backward, falling over one of my boxes and landed on top of it. I quickly hopped back up and looked toward her to see if she had gotten up. She hadn't.

One by one, I picked up the boxes and placed them on her front porch until there was nothing left, and even though I wanted to say something to convince her to forgive me, I placed my hand on her doorknob and closed the front door behind me. Looking back at the closed door, I expected to see Nitrah standing there telling me she wanted to give us another try. But after five minutes of standing still, I realized that she wasn't coming to the door to get me. I didn't think she would ever look at me the same, and for the first time since I met her, I knew in my heart that she did not want to be with me.

CHARMAINE WRIGHT

August 2005

I opened my closet door and began to throw clothes into an empty box. I didn't even bother to fold them because I was in more than a rush to see it all boxed away. Weeks had passed now since I had cut the rest of the world out of my life, and in my gut, I felt that the storm hadn't even started yet. I needed to get away, and I needed to do it now.

I walked back into my living room, making sure to not tumble over the brown boxes that now decorated my place when I heard a knock at my door. I debated on answering the door because whoever it was, I wasn't trying to speak or see anyone at this point.

"I know you are in there." I rolled my eyes and cursed under my breath as I heard Joyclyn's aggravating voice. *This bitch just won't let me be.*

"What do you want, Joy?" I yelled through the door. I had given her money not too long ago, and I was hoping that by the time she got the nerve to bother me again I would be long gone.

"You know what I want. You haven't been answering your phone lately, and now it's cut off. Seems you're trying to hide from me. You know I can still tell your little secret."

I started to feel pushed up against the wall again when she brought on a new threat. But now more than ever I just wanted to slam her head into a wall. I pulled open my front door and was halted by another familiar voice.

"Joy, isn't it? I think you can leave now, because that threat is no longer going to work," the voice said to Joyclyn's back.

Joyclyn turned around and came face to face with the reality that she already knew of. "Oh, so when did you get back in town? Still going after married men, huh?"

Monica pushed passed Joyclyn and proceeded to give me a bear hug. I must admit I did miss her ever since Dahlia had her moved to North Carolina. She was my best friend and had been since we were kids. To say she was family was saying it lightly because it was like we shared the same blood.

Monica turned back toward Joyclyn and said, "Yeah, Char told me about your little threats, but if you're smart, you would walk your skinny ass off this here front porch and keep it moving."

"Don't test me, Monica. I know about you and Char's little scam to win over Tim. I wonder how little Ms. Jazz would feel if she knew all along that Char was fucking Tim. Hmmm, I wonder …" Joyclyn said folding her arms and tapping her foot.

"Come back later tonight. I'll have some money for you." I slammed the door in Joyclyn's face, pulling Monica in by her arm. When the door closed, I felt like my world as I used to know it was back the way it used to be.

It was a hot summer's evening in Winston-Salem, but that didn't stop Monica from knocking on my mother's door asking for me to make a run with her. At sixteen we were both built like grown women, both losing our virginity at 13. I had yelled back into the house telling my mother I would return in a while.

She didn't bother to reply, as I knew she was passed out with another bottle of hard liquor once again. I slipped on my sandals and ran after Monica, who had taken her older brother's car.

"Tyler let you borrow his car?" I asked stupidly, knowing the answer was no.

"Girl, please, Tyler's up in the house with Jessica, and you know when they start fucking they don't come out for hours. So we're good." She leaned under the driver's seat and pulled out a plastic bag.

"Where did you get this chronic from?"

"Al gave me some. That's where we headed to now, and you know his boy Kevin is there just waiting to tap your ass. You gon' give him some tonight?"

Laughing at Monica as I took a cigar in my hand and started to empty its contents to replace it with the weed, I said, "Kevin's fine butt can have this ass."

"Good, 'cause I ain't trying to leave until my pussy is well taken care of."

"Yeah, whatever. Will you slow down? I'm trying to roll this weed, and I'm not trying to drop any."

We made it to Al's house in twenty minutes, and I took the cigar I had just filled with weed and slipped it into my pocket. Walking up to the door, I heard music playing. Monica asked him if his boy Kevin was here. He nodded his head yes.

"You ladies go upstairs. Monica, show Charmaine my brother's room right next door. We'll be up there in a minute."

Giggling, we followed his instructions and ran up the stairs. "OK, girl, don't be knocking on my door saying you ready if Kevin is a one-minute brother," Monica said laughing.

"Trust, if he a minute brotha, you will know." I walked in and took in the room, noticing a few posters on the wall and dirty clothes sprawled across the floor. Then I sat on the edge of the bed and waited for Kevin to come up.

I took the weed out of my pocket and placed it on the desk, hoping that we would smoke it after we were done. A minute rolled by and I heard feet coming up the stairs. My insides started to bubble over with anticipation.

Then I heard voices. That must be Kevin and Al, I thought. I could tell that Al had just opened his door. Next, I heard muffled voices, so I got up and placed my ear against the door.

"What the hell is he doing here, Al?" I heard Monica yell. Something in her voice wasn't right, and then I heard her scream, "Char, get out of the house."

I jumped back and pulled open the bedroom door to see what was wrong. Stepping into the door frame I felt a hand push my body backward.

"Hey, Char, what's up?" It was Kevin. Then I heard Monica's voice muffled at this point. I could tell that her mouth was being covered.

"Kevin, hey, what's going on?" I brought my hand to my chest where he pushed me, and I felt that I had shrunk three feet when I saw two silhouettes behind him. "Who is that?"

"I'm glad you two bitches came over, because we wanna fuck," I heard one of the others say.

"Wait, it isn't that kind of party. Just let me and Monica leave."

One guy stepped toward me and I could now see his face. He was in his twenties, but I didn't know him. "Can't you hear Monica is already enjoying herself with Al and my boys? Don't you want to do the same?"

I turned to close the bedroom door but was stopped when one of them wrapped his arm around my neck and pushed me further inside. "Yo', I'll call you when I'm almost done." He kicked the door shut with his foot and pushed me down on the bed.

"Open those fucking legs, Char. I heard how you like it."

"No, please, don't do this." I stood up, but was knocked back when he struck me in my face, causing me to fall back on the bed. His hands ran over my shorts, and made their way to my button. I squirmed and kicked, but he was so much stronger than me, and I could tell I was losing this battle when I felt him rip my shorts off. Then he angrily pulled my panties to the side, jabbing his fingers inside of me.

My screams were cut short when I saw someone else enter the room and place his hand over my mouth, using his other hand to grab my breast. I could feel a breeze where my panties used to be as he pushed open my legs so hard that I felt my inner thigh pop. I screamed out in agony. The worst pain was when he rammed himself in me, jabbing himself in me so hard I could feel his pelvic bone attack my groin.

I grabbed the bedsheets hard as he tried to turn my body over. Then he told the other one to help flip me over. Two against one was no contest as I thrown in the air and tossed on my stomach. Next, a burning pain shot up my spin. I cried out for them to stop, screaming that it hurt, now realizing that the other one was inside of my butt, ripping me a new hole. Blood gushed down my thighs.

Soon, I thankfully lost consciousness.

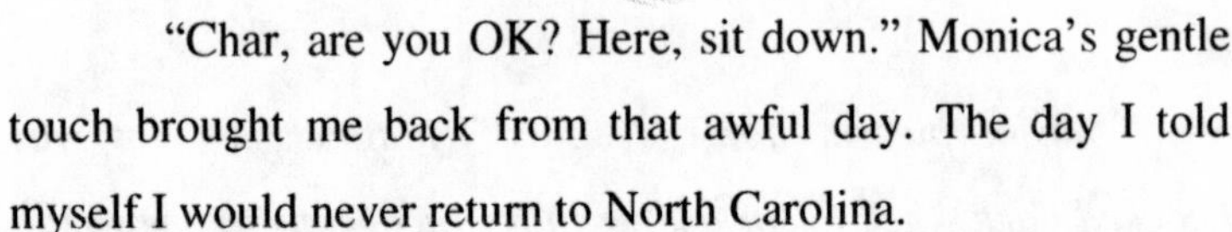

"Char, are you OK? Here, sit down." Monica's gentle touch brought me back from that awful day. The day I told myself I would never return to North Carolina.

I didn't notice that I had tears in my eyes until my vision started to blur. "I'm sorry, girl. My mind took me to a place I didn't want to remember." I could tell that Monica was trying to recall what could have me upset so quickly. So many bad things had happened to me that I didn't want her calling out every single thing.

"The night with Kevin and Al." The mention of their names changed her entire demeanor.

"Yeah, I don't want to think about that night." Just like me, Monica was raped by more than five men that night. Because of that experience, I cannot bear children and Monica took on a new mission to never trust another man.

I guess you could say it was easy to get her to seduce Tim for me. Crazy thing, I know, since I was the one in love with Tim. I had been since the day we started the scam on

Troy. I would secretly have sex with him while he pursued Jazzaray.

I hated their relationship and hated the fact that she gave the man I loved so much, something I couldn't—a child. I tried to move on with my life and forget all the evil shit I had done when I was in the company of Monica. But when Tim married Jazz, I knew I had to get him back, but he couldn't know that I was the one who told Terrance about him. Which is why Terrance attacked Jazz in the first place, and that it was truly my fault that she killed him in self-defense.

I couldn't let my girls know who I really was because moving away from North Carolina and Monica was supposed to be the end of that chapter. I was a new person now. Which is why I took on the role as a consoling friend. Shoot, I thought marrying Bobby would make Tim jealous, but at the end of the day, all he ever wanted from me was sex.

Now I was running away from it all. I was only 25, and I knew I could start over somewhere else. Just Monica and me.

Picking my phone up on its third ring, I said, "Hello."

"Sis, you won't believe who's at Char's house," I heard Joyclyn say.

"Joy, I don't give a damn who's at Char's house. Apparently me and her aren't cool any more either."

"Monica!"

"Monica who?"

"Your old assistant Monica."

Sitting up in my bed totally confused, I started to recall who Monica was. In a split second, I remembered very well. She was my assistant who slept with Tim and destroyed Jazz and Tim's marriage. Now the million-dollar question was why she was at Char's.

"I don't get it," I said.

"It looks like they're old friends to me."

"Wait a minute now, how do you know?"

I heard her stumble over her words before saying, "I keep in touch with Char for Darius, and you know she still watches him every now and then," she said referring to her son Darius. I knew she was lying but overlooked it.

"Let me call you back, sis." I hung up my phone and sat with my chin in my hand, confused. *What connection would Charmaine and Monica have?*

I flipped open my cell phone and scrolled down to the number I was looking for. Dialing, I took a deep breath and waited for him to answer.

"Yo', what up?" Tim said.

"Hey, it's me, Dahlia."

"Yeah, what's up, Dahlia? What are you doing calling my phone?"

"Look, I know it ain't none of my business, but something ain't right about this situation, and I got a strong feeling you got something to do with it."

"Oh, really? What situation? Are we talking about you and Troy?"

"No, Tim, I'm talking about Monica."

"Monica!"

"Yes, your girl Monica."

"I ain't thought about her since she left. Why are you bringing her up?"

"She's over Char's house right now."

"Charmaine's house?" he repeated, confused.

"Yes, Tim, Charmaine's house."

"I don't get it. Why would she be over there, and why …"

When he cut off I could tell he was thinking about something and that this situation was starting to make sense to him. "Hey, Tim, are you still there?"

"Dahlia, let me call you back." Before I could protest I heard a dial tone. Quickly, I pulled on my sneakers, dialing Troy's number at the same time.

"Hey, I don't have time to talk right now," he said before I could say hi. He had been blowing me off ever since Nitrah and Jazz found out about us.

"I don't care what you are doing. Drop it and head over to Charmaine's house. Something is about to go down, and I think your boy Tim may want you there."

"Charmaine's house? I'm confused. Where has she been?"

"Troy, stop asking questions and get in your truck. I'm on my way over there right now." I flipped the phone shut and suddenly stopped in my tracks. *Tim, Monica, Charmaine all together and no one knows why.* I smiled to myself as I opened my phone and scrolled down to her number this time. I also thought she needed to be included on this little trip too.

Walking into the house, I carried a sleeping Tim Junior up the stairs to his room. Laying him down on the bed, I pulled the covers up to his chest.

"Hey, baby," I heard Maxwell's voice from behind me. I sighed from a little annoyance and turned to give him a weak smile. I promised my mother that I would give it a try with Maxwell, because I knew in my heart that he was a good man. But I also felt like packing up everything I owned and moving out.

"Hey, Maxwell." I saw him flinch at my greeting. I quickly picked up on the fact that I called him Maxwell. It was too formal, since I always called him Max.

"You guys want to order some food and we stay in tonight and watch some movies?"

"No, Maxwell, I have some work to do and the kitchen is in need of a cleaning." I squeezed my way past him in the door frame, making sure not to allow my body to brush up against his.

"I already did the kitchen, the bathroom downstairs, and the living room. I just want you to relax tonight, baby." I could feel him try to reach toward me and squeeze my shoulder to show some sign of affection, but I quickly dodged his hand.

He sighed and placed his hands in his pockets. I jogged down the stairs when I heard my phone beep. Flipping it open, I saw a text from Dahlia. Rolling my eyes, I clicked to open it.

Dahlia: I'm telling u as a former friend to get ur butt over 2 Charmaine's house. Ur old friend Monica is there.

I angrily laughed at her message and closed my phone. As messy as the message was, it bothered the hell out of me that it didn't make sense.

"Baby, is you OK?"

I stood in the same spot I was in when I read the message a second time, not realizing that I hadn't moved. Jumping out of my trance, I looked toward Max, and my emotions must have been written all over my face.

"Max, watch Junior for me. I got to make a run."

"Baby, where are you running off to?" I grabbed my keys and ignored his question. I knew that I shouldn't have taken Dahlia's message to heart, but I did, and I was curious to know what she meant.

I must have broken all state traffic laws as I ran through red and yellow lights and only halfway stopped at the stop signs. Time was not on my side, and I wanted to make sure I made it to Char's house in time for whatever awaited for me there. I pulled up onto Char's street and turned off my headlights. It was well after nine, and I didn't want anyone to see me pulling up.

I parked my car a couple houses down and across the street from Charmaine's house. That's when I noticed Tim's truck in the driveway. *Why would Tim and Monica be over at Char's house?*

I turned off the engine and sat back in my seat agitated. I wasn't sure what to expect from this meeting. Why care if Monica was here anyhow? Tim wasn't my husband anymore. When I started to question myself and debate about leaving or not, I glanced over and saw Char's front door swing open.

Tim walked out and was obviously upset and yelling at someone in the house. I heard a women's voice yell, "I love you." *What? Monica and Tim are in love?*

Starting to get mad at myself for allowing myself back into the web of Tim's lies, I placed my hand on the key and started the ignition. That is—until I saw the woman step out and realized that it wasn't Monica declaring her love—it was Char.

"Char, get the hell out of my face with that shit. You knew from the beginning what was up, and you pull this shit and you take Jazz away from me. This is some bull," Tim yelled.

My mouth dropped in disbelief. This could not be happening. No way was I seeing my best friend declare she was in love with my husband all along. *How long? When did this start? How long have they been betraying me?*

My hand gripped my door frame as I swung it open. I could feel my heart beating so fast that the pulse was running down my arm and vibrating through my fingers. I slammed the door behind me so loud that it made a huge thud and startled every one of them.

Tim jerked and looked toward my car and proceeded to squint his eyes in an effort to see if it was really me. *Yes, it's me, motherfucker.*

Charmaine covered her mouth and said, "Oh my God, Jazz, what are you doing here?"

"Well, this reunion just got better," I heard Monica say as she took her first step onto Charmaine's porch.

Rushing toward me with his arms extended, Tim started to sound like Eric Benét, begging, "Jazz, baby, please. Wait! Let me explain. It's not what it seems."

Agitation, betrayal, and confusion had already consumed me as I balled up my fist and swung it at Tim's head, landing directly in the middle of his cheek. He covered his face in defense and dodged my next hit.

He tried to grip me, but I ran past him heading directly for my new target: Char.

Backing up against her bushes I screamed, "How long, Charmaine? How long have you been fucking Tim?"

Monica walked up toward me and stopped when I yelled, "Bitch, come near me and I will kill you." I guess the anger in my eyes led her to believe that, and she took a step back.

I looked back toward Char and yelled my question again. She started to cry hysterically. I could give a damn about the tears she cried because for the first time, I didn't recognize the person I saw. For the first time, I hated the person before me. She was my friend, my confidante, the one I could always lean on. She gave me sound advice on how to handle these situations, and now I am staring her in the face because of her betrayal.

"Since the very beginning, Jazz. I'm sorry, but I never wanted you to know."

Completely baffled at this point, I was ready to cut someone. I turned and looked at Tim, staring him dead in the eyes as I asked Char my next question. "What's *from the very beginning*, Char? When exactly?"

Tim was shaking his head for Char to shut up. I imagine he knew that once the truth came out, there was never going to be a relationship between us—as lovers or friends.

Charmaine cried out, "When we all saw them in Bennigan's Restaurant all those years ago. I started up with him when Dahlia and Nitrah started that scam. He was mine first; he just chose you." My mind raced back to the night we had met Troy and Tim. The night we had gotten in a fight with Sarah and Kia at Arlington Lake. That was the night Nitrah first met Troy, the night I first laid eyes on Tim.

I laughed in disgust. "You mean to tell me, Tim, that from the beginning, you were fucking Char when I was attacked by Terrance, when I was pregnant with Junior, when I walked down the aisle to marry you, when you were begging me to take you back after fucking Monica. All this time you were just playing me. You never changed. Damn, you're worse than Troy." I glanced over and saw Troy standing on the street curb. Tim followed my eyes and noticed him too. Then Tim dropped his head in shame.

"You know what, Char? You were never a friend." I noticed the boxes that covered her living room. "You packing and leaving, huh? Well, get the fuck out of town and don't even bother looking back." I raised my hand and slapped her once for the road. Then I looked toward Monica and thought about punching her ass out too. But why would I be mad at her? Tim was the one who betrayed me.

"Jazz, baby." Tim tried to follow me to my car. I turned around and screamed for him to leave me alone. "Troy, get your man before I kill him."

Turning quickly, I ran to my car and buried my head into the steering wheel and cried for what seemed like an hour but was only a few seconds. I glanced up and placed my key in the ignition when I noticed Dahlia sitting in her car across the street. I couldn't read her expression, but I could care less. She could go to hell too.

I placed my car in gear and sped off into the night. Not wanting to go home and not having any friends to lean on, I heard my phone beep and saw it was a message from Dahlia.

Dahlia: For what it's worth, I'm sorry.

I threw the phone closed and headed to the only friend's house I knew was suffering from a broken heart too: Nitrah.

I was way too embarrassed to walk into a restaurant and eat alone. But with no one to hang out with and no one to date that was just what I was about to do. I told the hostess that it was just me and I would like to sit at the bar. Maybe I could blend in with the crowd, and no one would really notice I was eating alone.

Once I was seated, I started to rethink my idea of ordering take out. I picked up the menu and proceeded to act as if I were interested in its contents. One thing about eating out alone is you have no one to talk to.

"I know you're not eating alone," a voice said.

I ignored the voice and imagined he wasn't talking to me, but I realized how mistaken I was when the person said, "Nitrah, right?"

I turned to face his voice and smiled. "Yeah, and you look familiar."

" Marlo. We met at Denim's sis's graduation dinner at his folks' place this past summer." He extended his hand, and I shook it.

How can I forget a tall dark specimen like you? "Oh, right. I forgot about that for a minute," I lied.

"Oh, yeah, well, Nitrah, can I join you? I was going to order from the bar and leave, but now that I see I may have company, I think I want to change those plans."

I had told myself I wouldn't date … but dinner wouldn't hurt. "Sure, why not?"

He sat at the barstool next to me and threw a twenty-dollar bill on the bar. "Yo', bartender, let me get a Crown and Coke and get the lady here whatever she wants." He glanced toward me and winked. I took in his soft-looking lips, broad shoulders, huge hands, and the confidence of a king. *Ummm, I wonder …*

It's only dinner, right? It's not like I was going to have a repeat of Troy again.

I had one too many. But Darrell's company was so worth it. After four drinks, I managed to call myself a cab and have the driver drop me off home, but not before placing Darrell's number in my phone. I was definitely going to link back up with him again.

I paid the driver for the ride and proceeded to get out of the car when I noticed Jazz's car in my driveway. I dragged my feet and walked up to her driver-side window and tapped on it. "Jazz, what's up?"

She rolled down her window, and I noticed her bloodshot eyes. She said, "Nitrah, I need to vent. Can I talk to you?"

I pulled open her door with concern and said, "Jazz, come on, girl. Now you know you can talk to me."

Inside, I turned on the living-room light and plopped down on the couch, throwing my shoes to the floor. Jazz followed behind me, getting just as comfortable.

"Is Nina with your mother tonight?"

"She's with Troy's mom. So tell me what's up. What done happened now?"

With the most concerned look I had ever seen on Jazzaray's face, she said, "Nitrah, after all these years, Dahlia can betray you and then, out of the blue, Charmaine can betray me. When I say we never truly had good friends, I mean it."

Sitting upward from my position on the couch I placed my head in my hands and said, "I know what the bitch Dahlia did, but of all people, what did Charmaine do?"

When she repeated the story of Tim and Char being together all of these years, I damn near wanted to spit venom. Without a doubt in my mind, this was the ultimate no-no. What friend does this to another friend?

I leaned back on my couch and curled my legs up to my chest, almost forgetting that Jazz was here. I didn't know when they started to flow, but when I felt wetness on my hand, I looked down and noticed the teardrops.

Jazz whispered, "Why are you crying?"

"I'm just sad, that's all."

She sighed and leaned back on the couch and proceeded to let her tears fall as well. "First, I kill Terrance; then I lose Tim; now Maxwell cheats; and to top this all off, the four girls I once loved and viewed as my sisters are no more."

I added, "First, it was losing Denim; then Troy; then Michael; and then Troy again; and when all was said and done, my girls betray me." I laughed and said, "Jazz, what you got to tell me now?"

She laughed weakly and said, "Just that I love you, girl. No matter what, don't do me like they did us. Promise?" She held out her pinky and implied for me to pinky swear. I took my pinky and wrapped it around hers.

"I promise."

Two Weeks Later

"Oh, hey, Jazz, I just got out of the shower. I'm about to leave early for the Lyrical Lounge today. Are you at the store already?"

"No, I have one of my employees there. I needed to check on you. Max is going to be busy all weekend, so why don't you let one of your managers run the place and take a break? I know ever since the altercation went down with Dahlia and Troy, you need to get away."

"Just the opposite. I need to work."

"Can you please stop being bigheaded? We all single gals here; we could hit up Florida with your sis Raven. Even your sisters would be willing to get down right about now."

"Wait a minute. My line is beeping." I clicked over the line and before I had the chance to say hello, a female voice said, "Nitrah? Is this Nitrah?"

"Yes, this is Nitrah. Who is this?"

"I just thought you should know Troy isn't where he says he is. Get Nina and get out of town for a while. You know your girl Dahlia has it in for you."

"Who the hell is this, and where is Troy?"

"Just remember what I said. Your girl Dahlia has it in for you." The line went dead. I hurried and clicked back over.

"You know I hate when you put me on hold," Jazz complained.

"I am about to fuck somebody up," I yelled.

"Why? Who was that?"

"Call Tim and ask him where the fuck Troy's at. I'm tired of this shit. I want to confront him once and for all."

"OK, let me go get my bat and let's pay Dahlia a visit while we're at it."

"See you in twenty minutes." I hung up the phone and raced to my closet, pulling my hair into a ponytail and putting on my running shoes. Enough was enough. I was about to confront the one person I wanted to be with.

Hopping in my car, I read a text from Jazz saying that Tim said Troy was over at Dahlia's. That's funny because in a weak moment, Troy was in my bed last night. I texted her back to tell her to meet me there now. She replied and said she was already on the way.

I noticed Jazz walk up to my car. "I got the bat."

I hopped out of my car and snatched the bat out of her hand and ran up to Troy's truck. I screamed, "You want to play both sides, Troy?"

Bam! His taillight was history.

"You want to play with people's hearts now, do you?"

Bam! His back window shattered, spraying sparkling shrapnel everywhere.

"How about this, Troy? You want to fuck Dahlia and me at the same time?"

Bam! His driver-side window was nonexistent.

I looked up and noticed Dahlia's front door swing open. Jazz immediately took noticed and proceeded to block Troy from getting to me.

"Hey, Troy, how about we all just have a fucking threesome?"

Bam! His front windshield looked like his back window.

Troy yelled, "What the hell are you doing, Nitrah?" He grabbed Jazz's arms and swung her to the ground, then raced toward me. I immediately ran around the other side of the truck and headed straight for Dahlia's car, my next target.

"I'm redecorating your and your bitch's cars. Can't you tell?" I swung the bat at Dahlia's car now.

Bam! Dahlia's driver-side window exploded.

Jazz jumped up off the ground when she saw Dahlia running out of the house. I wanted to get one more hit in before Troy could catch up to me, so I slammed the bat into her front windshield. *Bam!*

"What are you doing, Nitrah?" Dahlia screamed. She had the nerve to walk outside in one of Troy's T-shirts. In the blink of an eye, Jazz ran toward Dahlia and slapped her hard in the face.

Troy rushed up to me and proceeded to yell in my face about the damage I just did to his car. It was as if everything went into slow motion as I glanced back and forth at my friends fighting in Dahlia's front yard and the man I once loved with my entire heart looked at me with such disgust. *How the hell can he look at me this way?* I was the victim, not the other way around.

Raising my hands up in frustration, I yelled, "Everyone just stop!"

Instantly, Troy stopped talking and Jazz let go of her grip on Dahlia and looked up at me. I had just realized that I was so over this situation. This wasn't love. Love didn't stab you in the back. Love didn't sleep with your best friend. Love wouldn't cause you to lose yourself and your identity. Love loves you back, and this just wasn't it.

I wanted to be loved at this moment and to be held and spoken to in a tender, loving voice. I wanted to look up into the eyes of the man who loved me and feel secure that he would never hurt me.

But looking at Troy, I started to recap everything we had been through and came to realize that he had hurt me on too many occasions, and I had done the same to him. Was that love?

Was I truly in love with Denim? Did my best friends truly love me and have my back? When I noticed that my answers to my questions were no, I started to understand all of this drama.

Will love ever know me?

"Jazz, let's go. I'm done with this situation. Fuck it. Y'all two can have each other because truth be told, you deserve each another."

"Nitrah, I'm sorry," Troy said.

Rolling my eyes I said, "Troy, I really don't want to go there with you. This situation with her," I said pointing to Dahlia, "is fucked up. But hey, it is what it is. I'm tired of loving you and not being loved. I'm tired of wondering when we're going to get back together. I'm tired of hoping and praying and wishing. I'm just tired, Troy. And for once, I'm at peace. I'm at peace with your bullshit. I'm at peace with you fucking her. I'm at peace with me not wanting you. I'm at peace with us not being a family. For once in my life, it's about me and no one else. You, Troy, are the last thing on my mind." I pointed my finger deep into his chest and pushed him out of my path.

I looked toward Jazz and said, "Go get in your car. Let's go home. There's nothing here for us to discuss."

JAZZARAY MEADOWS

I guess you can say that I had moved on. Once I was able to really think about Rayne and Maxwell together, I knew that I couldn't truly walk away. He was the love of my life. He was there when I was at my lowest, and to be honest, I believe he would never intentionally hurt me.

All in all, it didn't take me long to agree on reconciling with him. Especially after seeing the continued hurt Nitrah went through with Troy. I knew that deep down, I wouldn't grow through pain like that with Maxwell. And now since he told me Rayne is no longer in town, I felt that I could breathe a sigh of relief.

Life after that got easier, and without anyone else to lean on, Nitrah and I just grew closer. With Charmaine now a faded memory, we had to be each other's backbone. My relationship with Tim was nonexistent except for when it came to Junior, and for once, I accepted the fact that he had done the ultimate betrayal. What was done was done.

It wasn't easy at first for Nitrah to move on, but she did, and I was glad to see that she was casually dating and not taking everything serious. She even gave up the sex with Denim. Not even I would have guessed that.

I started to think back to one of my lowest moments in my life when I sought counseling and when my therapist sent me out on that mission to face my fears. I was to go back to the apartment where I had killed Terrence and leave my fears behind. Whatever my fears consisted of, I was to write them down on a piece of paper and leave it at the door of the apartment where my life had changed. Funny how now when I think about it, everything I wrote on that piece of paper came to pass in one shape or another.

First, it was find a job that I love, leave Tim for good, get rid of the friends who are poison, let go of sadness, be open to new love, forgive myself for killing Terrence, and go to church more often. Okay, I hadn't tackled the last one just yet, but I knew deep down that I had tackled all the rest. I no longer had panic attacks, I trusted my heart with Maxwell, and I could look at Tim and not want to kill him.

Life was good, and for once, I felt that I knew love, and love sure knew the hell out of me.

JOYCLYN JONES

So did my plan work? At the end of the day, I guess you can say I got what I wished for. Not that I hated Charmaine and all that; it's just I wanted to have free money and since she held skeletons in her closet, she was an easy target.

I didn't expect her to just up and move, but hey, that's just what she did. I held on to her secrets for a long time before I allowed her to know that I knew. Back when I got pregnant with Darius by Eric, who was my sister Dahlia's boyfriend at the time, I was kicked out of Dahlia's house and had to move in with Charmaine.

The many conversations she had with a person I came to know as Monica started to interest me. It wasn't long before she was confessing her love for Tim to Monica, and that gave me power in a sense.

But hey, all is well now. No one really knows all the details anyhow. Not to say I'm going to go out and yell them to the world, 'cause hey, Charmaine is long gone now. Even my sister doesn't hang out with Nitrah and Jazz anymore. So I guess I can just forget about all the dirty little secrets that were never told.

I guess it doesn't matter anyhow, because my big break is about to come. Just when I thought my connection to Nitrah wasn't worth a damn, lo and behold, Denim starts to produce an album for a new artist named JL, and this gives me a great leeway into his life, if you know what I mean. So I started to put that plan in motion. I needed a man, and a man with money is just what I needed.

Who knows? He may just be my connection to getting the hell out of Fort Worth.

Stay Tuned for Joyclyn's story in

He's My Favorite Mistake

Coming

Summer 2012

Also available from

Delphine Publications

Luck of the Draw

by

Anna Black

Chapter One

Kennedy wasn't in the mood for going out that Saturday evening. She had just gotten off from a long day of work at the jewelry store and she was exhausted. Since she owned the store, certain packages that came in could only be verified by her, so that day had her mentally and physically tired. She drove home telling herself, 'I can't wait to put my feet up and sip on a glass of something that will help me relax.'

She walked in the door, leaving everything she carried into the house in the foyer, and told herself that she'd get it later. She climbed the steps to her bedroom with a smile on her face because she finally reached her destination to a peaceful place, but her best friend, Cherae, was at her door within minutes, pressing her to go out with them to the club. She took off her shoes, trying to ignore Cherae as she took off her clothes, and then she slipped into her comfy robe.

"Come on, girl, all you need is a shower and you'll be refreshed. Teresa said she'd be here by 11:30 and that will give you plenty of time to get some rest and be ready. You work at a jewelry store, Kay, not on a farm, so you can't be that tired," she whined.

Kennedy knew that she was in for a battle if Teresa was there, too, in her ear to go out. She knew that would be a no win situation. They always cornered her and talked her into going out with them, even when she really didn't want to go. The thing was; they'd drink more than she did and they knew she'd be sober enough to drive their drunken behinds home, so she knew it wasn't them really wanting her to go, they just wanted to get their drink on.

"Okay, man, damn. I will go, but don't think I'm driving because after the day I just had, I want to get some liquor in me and I'm not driving you drunk heifers home this time. I'm the one who's going to be in the back seat passed out, understood?"

"Yes, yes," Cherae said with excitement.

"Now, get out of here so I can rest my nerves before Ree gets here," Kennedy playfully ordered.

"No problem, madam. I will let you be, but you know I'm gon' be right back up here to make sure you are getting ready, and, Kay, can I borrow your little blue Donna Karen purse? I need it for tonight," she asked.

Kennedy wanted to say no because Cherae always borrowed her things, but she was too sweet to say no, and it wasn't like she was going to need it.

"Yea, it's in the closet on the bottom rack, and when you come back up to so-call check on me, you better have me a glass of wine in your hand, too," Kennedy said with a smile.

Cherae was her girl, no matter what, and she loved her to death. She did a lot for Cherae, and it didn't bother her one bit. She just wondered when Cherae was going to get herself together and stop being so needy. She was so dependant and Kennedy didn't understand how she settled when she had so much opportunity to be so much better. She had no kids or excuses to hold her back from doing something with her life, and she wasn't paying Kennedy a dime to live there. Cherae just thought her looks would land her a rich man and after thirty-four years of trying to land a millionaire, she was still unlucky to accomplish that mission.

Kennedy walked into her massive walk-in closet and it didn't take long for her to find something to wear. She had so many clothes, shoes, purses, and hats; she didn't have to go through a million and one channels to look fabulous. Kennedy was a plump woman, full-figured society would say, but at a size sixteen, there was nothing bad anyone could say about her. She was conservative in some ways, but she knew how to turn on the sexy.

She loved going out with her girlfriends and even though she was the heavier sister, she still turned a few heads when they went out together. She knew she was gorgeous because her daddy taught her that. She never felt more or less beautiful than her two girls, but she did know for a fact that they had it going on.

Teresa was an averaged size woman, not fat at all Kennedy thought to herself when she'd hear her complaining about how she gained a pound or two. Teresa stood about five feet and at one hundred and thirty pounds, she looked good in everything she wore because she was curvy. Her hips and butt filled her jeans to a tee while her B cupped breast couldn't go without a padded bra. She had pretty, light brown skin and it was smooth and clear. Her short and sassy hair style would always receive compliments from women and men, and it looked good on her round face.

As pretty as Kennedy thought Teresa was, she hardly understood how she always had man trouble. Kennedy realized, after meeting and getting to know Teresa that looks had absolutely nothing to do with getting a man because Teresa's bright smile and gorgeous figure didn't make a man stay with her, and most of her men turned out to be crazy.

Then, there was Cherae, the bombshell of the trio; the head turner and show stopper. She knew she looked good and didn't try to front like she wasn't the bomb. She was high yellow with long, straight, dark hair that she kept blonde highlights in. Women swore her hair was a weave. Her body was tight because she worked out five days a week to maintain her size four frame. Her eyes were hazel naturally, but most people thought they were fake. She had a pear shaped face with a little cute nose, and since she never knew who her dad, Kennedy would sometimes joke that her daddy was of another race because her momma was Kennedy's complexion and had a big nose. Cher was five feet two inches tall and although she was slim, her body was shaped perfect with a C cupped breast size that could go easily without a bra for support and she never looked like a skinny girl in jeans.

Cherae didn't have relationship issues and getting a man was never one of her downfalls, meeting a man with a lot of money was what caused her problems. She had plenty of marriage proposals and dated numerous men, but she just didn't have it upstairs. She was a beauty with no brains, looking for a free ride.

Of Kennedy's two friends, Teresa had all the good qualities that a woman could have, including a sweet personality. She was always honest and tried to always be straight up with folks. She never acted like she was better than others and most of all, she was fair. She was the cool head of the group and wouldn't argue with anyone over anything at anytime. She and Kennedy were close and spent more time together because they worked together.

They met about six years ago when Kennedy took over one of her dad's jewelry stores.

Teresa had no experience nor did she know anything about the jewelry business, but she was the only person that Kennedy liked when she interviewed. She and Kennedy hit it off and realized that they had a lot in common, except for the knowledge of diamonds, silver, and gold. So, after she promised Kennedy she would learn the business, Kennedy hired her and was so glad she did.

Cherae, on the other hand, was a different case. She and Kennedy had been friends their entire lives, and for so long Kennedy had told her that she was not going to be able to live off her good looks, but Cherae, being as irresistible as she thought she was, had men paying her way for everything. She used men to her advantage, but got caught up on a wealthy, older gentleman that put her up in a nice condo downtown. He was married but that didn't mean a thing to Cher because he was very rich and had his own company, and as long as Cher took trips with him and filled in as his woman when he wanted a show piece on his arm, he took care of her. That lasted a couple years 'til he found a younger superstar to cater to and he dropped her ass, and she had to move in with Kennedy.

Kennedy wasn't so torn up about it because she loved Cherae like a sister. She was an only child and she and Cherae were practically raised together, being that they met in the second grade. When they graduated high school they parted briefly but after the first year of college away from home, Kennedy was home sick and she went back home to attend school near her family, so she and Cherae were right back together. Once Kennedy got her Masters, her daddy decided it was time for her to take over the store that he ran and owned for twenty-four years. Kennedy was honored to take over and have her own store because her two cousins ran two other locations that belonged to her uncles, Kendal and Keith.

They were a close knit family, too, and they were all wealthy and accepted Cher as family until Cher dated her cousin, Kory, for a while and showed her natural simple ass. The family viewed her a little different, yet still respected her because she and Kennedy were so close. They were like "Two peas in a pod," Kennedy's daddy, Kenneth, would say, and told his nephews for Kennedy's sake to grin and bear her. Kennedy knew they didn't care for her much after the break up, but she figured she messed over Kory like she did all men because that was the norm for Cher. She warned Kory how Cher was prior, but no, he just had to have her and she tried to drain his pockets. Kennedy tried to stay out of their relationship and not take sides, but they always involved her, so she was not sad when they finally broke up.

CPSIA information can be obtained at www.ICGtesting.com
Printed in the USA
LVOW12s1450040214

372300LV00001B/164/P